Royally Married

By
Jill Boyce

ISBN: 978-1-956654-37-0

Dedication

For my husband, who loves, supports, and encourages me and for my children, who give me purpose, laughter, and joy. Also, for Holden, our rascal golden retriever, who provides abundant book fodder and epic cuddles.

Acknowledgments

I praise God, who whispered these stories to my heart and placed the perfect people along my writing path at the perfect time.

I thank my husband, children, family, and friends for their love and support.

I am grateful to my mentor and friend, Carrie Turansky, for her generous spirit and wisdom, and my publisher, Cynthia Hickey, for believing in my work.

I'm appreciative to Sherri Stewart, my editor for this book, who made the story shine and taught me a lot along the way.

I especially thank my mother, who passed away six years ago on the day of my daughter's birth. Her death inspired my first book, *Harte Broken*. She instilled in me the love of books and the desire to dream big. I love you, Mom.

My hope is my stories will provide comfort, laughter, and encouragement to my readers. May God bless you all.

Proverbs 29:25 Fear of man will prove to be a snare, but whoever trusts in the LORD is kept safe. (NIV)

Chapter 1

The petite woman waved the morning newspaper close enough to touch Claire's face. "Have you seen this?"

Her eyes flicked toward the offending picture, praying that the image had changed since she'd glanced at it previously. Nope—still there. She swallowed hard, looked up, and stared at her reflection in the mirror. "I saw it."

"Then you realize what a catastrophe this creates."

"Catastrophe might be an exaggeration, don't you think?"

"No, that's exactly what it is." Mademoiselle Couture pointed at the picture. "What would you call a picture of the freshly minted queen standing before the castle giving her first official public speech wearing—" the woman choked out the following words, "scrubs!" Mademoiselle closed her eyes and pinched the bridge of her nose. Her black bob shook as her whole body shuddered. "I have no words."

It sounded like she had words—and plenty of them. Claire smoothed her hands over the mermaid-silhouette wedding gown the fashion guru had insisted she try on at eight a.m. of all times. She should be in bed under a fluffy comforter, dreaming of coffee and chocolate—not gasping for each breath in this torture device. Why did the bride have to suffocate to get married? The groom got to wear a loose shirt and flat shoes. Claire hadn't dared take a single step in the sky-high heels Mademoiselle had required her to wear. "I couldn't help it. I had on that navy-blue suit you selected for the event, but the hospital called me at the last minute with an emergency. I was the only one available that could fix the patient's leg. Besides, I wore the hat you chose."

Mademoiselle shook the newspaper again as if she were strangling it. "That only made you look more ridiculous. Wearing a pillbox hat with those ratty, wrinkled scrubs and that lab coat—I—I can't—" She grabbed her chest and sank into a chair next to Claire, dropping her head into her hands.

Claire frowned. Mademoiselle Couture had never been in a state like this before. "I realize the wedding is soon, and you want me to look my best—what with me being a new monarch and all, but—"

The woman lifted her head, meeting Claire's eyes in the mirror. "No. It's more than that. You have to look perfect at all times. How people perceive you matters.

It's part of the job—to present yourself to the world in a manner suitable for a queen. You represent Evercliff Castle, the country of Amorley, and your family—especially your father. If he were alive today, what would he say? Hmm?"

Claire's stomach sank, but she nodded. "I don't want to disappoint anyone, especially not my family." She glanced at her reflection in the white lace concoction that resembled a straitjacket more than a wedding dress. Her eyes bounced toward the picture of herself on the front page of the newspaper, and she gulped. It did look bad. The only thing that could have been worse was if she had food stuck in her teeth or Wilson's muddy pawprints splattered across the front of her scrubs.

Mademoiselle Couture interrupted Claire's thoughts, "Do we have an understanding? You will defer to me in all things fashion from this point forward. No more unexpected wardrobe changes! I don't care if there's a medical emergency or anything else. No excuses."

Shuddering, Claire met the woman's gaze. "Agreed." She started to step down from the pedestal, anxious to slip out of the gown and into her comfortable pajama bottoms with the black hearts on them.

"One more thing." Mademoiselle Couture raised a finger in the air.

Claire froze in mid-retreat, in as much of a lunge as the constrictive dress would allow. "What's that?"

she uttered. *Please don't be another royal lesson.* She couldn't take any more today.

"That thing on top of your head—what do you call that?" The woman gestured with her nose toward the damp nest of hair piled on top of Claire's head.

Claire shifted her eyes toward the mirror once more, still half-hovering on the pedestal. "Uh, it's called a topknot. It's a bit messy because I didn't have time this morning. The hospital called me last night, and I went in to help as a favor, so by the time I arrived home, I only had time for a quick shower before I met with you and—"

Mademoiselle lifted a hand. "Please say no more. I cannot bear it. A queen cannot be seen wearing a—" Her lips puckered as she surveyed Claire's golden hair again before spitting out the words, "topknot." She scrunched her nose as if it pained her to say the word.

"I'm sorry. Next time you see me, I promise to have my hair fixed properly, and I won't be wearing scrubs. Honest." Claire pasted a smile on her face like the one her grandmother, the queen mother, had taught her.

Claire rubbed her forehead. Why did she always let people down no matter how hard she tried? There had been no time to rest between planning her wedding and learning to run the country. She'd hopped from one responsibility to the next since her coronation, and the crown weighed heavy on her head.'.

"I must be going." Mademoiselle abruptly stood

and clapped her hands.

A flurry of stiletto-heeled and sleek-haired assistants gathered around the intimidating woman. She barked a few orders in French, and they whisked away the unchosen wedding gowns, pins, and other fitting supplies. The most petite of them lifted the large leaning mirror that Mademoiselle had placed before Claire to use as she tried on gowns. The weight of the eight-foot-tall glass looked like it might crush the assistant, but to her credit, she didn't drop it. A rather large vein did bulge out of her forehead, however. Claire imagined the risk of a vein bursting paled compared to the prospect of angering Mademoiselle Couture. Claire snickered at the thought.

Mademoiselle Couture whipped her head around and glared at Claire. "What's so comical? It's not your furry friend, is it?" She scanned the room, ensuring that Wilson hadn't made a quiet appearance, ready to assault her and soil her outfit.

Claire couldn't fault the woman. She wouldn't put it past her adorable yet mischievous puppy to create a stir. Shaking her head, Claire stifled a giggle. "No, it's not Wilson. I'm sorry, I don't know why I laughed. I'm probably just tired." Not exactly a lie—her mother had drilled it into her head to be honest, but if the truth might hurt someone's feelings, it was wise to say what needed to be shared and no more.

Mademoiselle Couture studied Claire for a few more seconds, then shrugged. "Very well. I'm off. But don't forget—perfect. You always have to look perfect. I do not want to open another morning paper and see a photograph of you that causes me to choke on my coffee again. Oh, and don't let anything happen to that gown. Comprenez-vous?"

Oh no. Did Claire have to learn French now, too? She should have taken it in high school, but no—she took Latin to prepare for medical school. "Uh, sure. Oui. Guard the gown. Got it." *No pressure, no biggie.* Claire's neck muscles tightened as the next words tumbled out of her mouth, "And always be perfect."

Mademoiselle Couture gave a curt nod and click-clacked her way out of the room. The hive of assistants buzzed behind the queen bee, leaving Claire alone to consider her current situation.

Here she stood ensconced in the tightest garment she'd ever worn—and that was saying something considering the many monstrosities her grandmother had made her try on over the past several months. Skimming her hands over the lace, Claire noted how foreign the texture felt under her skin—not comfortable, that's for sure.

Sighing, Claire hiked up the bottom of the dress as much as it would allow. She stepped down off the pedestal, taking caution not to fall.

"Careful, ma'am. Watch your step." Albert appeared at her side, extending a hand to steady her.

She grabbed his arm and flashed him a grateful smile. "Thanks. They don't tell you that the hardest part about becoming the queen of a country will be the fashion…and the picture taking…and the speech giving."

The head of the household tipped his head upward. "Ah, I'm guessing you've either seen today's copy of *The Amorley Tribune* or had a run-in with Mademoiselle Couture."

Claire pointed a finger at him. "Bingo. You're two for two, Albie."

"Ma'am, if I may—" He paused, darting his eyes away from her.

Claire lifted a palm. "Please, go ahead. You can't say anything worse than she did. Let me guess—I'm making a mess of running Amorley, my father would be disappointed, and I'm not the perfect queen, doctor, or fiancée. Am I close?"

Albert frowned. "Not at all. I wanted to remind you of something." He paused before continuing, "Don't be afraid of people or what they think."

Claire snorted.

"I'm serious. True, you're the queen of Amorley, and there's a certain expectation of how you must behave and appear, but that's not what truly matters in life. The important thing is how you treat others— what's in your heart. Put your trust in God, and don't worry so much about what people think. It will wear you down."

Tears sprang to Claire's eyes. The salty moisture burned, and her throat tightened. Looking away, she avoided Albert's gaze. "I don't know about that," she whispered. "Right now, it seems like how I appear on paper matters most. According to today's representation, it's not looking good."

Albert released her hand and gave her an awkward pat on the shoulder. "Ma'am, I believe in you. You will become a great leader and handle this new role with poise and grace. If I may assist you on this journey in any way, do not hesitate to ask. What is it, you Americans say?" He tapped his chin. "I've got your back."

Claire chuckled at Albert's attempt at casual humor. "Thanks. I needed that."

He smiled, straightening his posture, then smoothed his black suit jacket and became serious again. "I have something that might cheer you up in the meantime."

She wiped away the last few tears and raised a brow. "Oh? What's that?"

Albert whistled, and all sixty pounds of Wilson, her loveable golden retriever, bounded into the room wearing a blue bow. "I taught him a new trick." The man turned to the puppy. "Wilson, sit."

For once, Claire's puppy obliged on the first attempt and sat rather than jumped on her white dress.

Claire's jaw fell. She took a few steps backward to see if the dog would remain in his obedient position.

He didn't budge.

Tilting her head to the side, Claire caught Albert's

gaze. "I'm impressed. What did you do?"

Albert smiled and rifled through his jacket pocket. When he removed his hand, he held a fistful of something. "Treats. Lots and lots of treats—oh, and something I believe the woman on television called a clicker. Such a funny word for it, but it does click." He glanced at the small device in his other hand.

Shaking her head, Claire smiled. Leave it to ole Albie to be the one to train the dog. She'd tried a few times herself and given up exasperated. "Well, whatever you did worked, so keep it up. At least now I'll have the perfect dog. One thing off the list to worry about, I suppose."

Albert took two steps forward and placed a hand on hers. "Nothing in life is ever perfect; in fact, it's often quite the opposite. That's what makes it so wonderful. Everyone is different—unique in their own way. If everything and everyone looked and behaved perfectly all the time, then this world would become quite boring indeed."

Claire sighed. "The queen mother, Mademoiselle Couture, the head of Parliament, and Oxmund Hospital don't see things that way. I must look, act, dress, and be perfect at all times, especially with the wedding approaching. There are a million ways I could embarrass the royal family and my father's legacy with all the events leading up to my wedding."

"Respectfully, ma'am, I disagree. Is there anything else I can do for you at present?"

Claire shook her head.

Albert turned his attention to Claire's puppy. "Sir Wilson, come."

The dog rose from his position and stretched his front and then hind legs in a series of yoga-like poses before trailing behind Albert, giving new meaning to 'downward dog.'

Claire watched as the pair vanished through the doorway and around the corner out of sight. With a downward glimpse of her dress, she pulled in as deep a breath as possible. "Ugh. I don't know if I'm going to survive this dress or this wedding, much less running the country. I guess it will be okay. Right?" she asked no one in particular.

Chapter 2

Imperfectly, Claire dashed into the dining room as Albert and the waitstaff gathered around the edge of the space, their arms filled with trays. "I'm sorry I'm late. You all could have started dinner without me."

The queen mother sat opposite Claire's empty chair at one end of the table. She lowered her glasses and looked over the top of them, sending her granddaughter "the look." "You are the queen now. We do not dine until you've been seated and taken your first bite. That's tradition, and we cannot upturn hundreds of years of it."

Claire slunk into her seat, breathless, and grabbed the napkin from the center of her plate. She shoved it in her lap and pushed back a few rogue strands of hair that had escaped from her bun. At least today, she had selected a respectable outfit—a black skirt, a button-up cream blouse, and even pantyhose and heels. Surely, her grandmother couldn't find fault with her appearance. Well, maybe the hair. However, after a day filled with wedding planning, hospital rounds, and a brief appearance at a local homeless shelter, Claire was surprised the bun had held at all. "Again, I apologize. I lost track of time, and Charlotte told me that we needed to leave at five, but, well—"

Claire's maternal grandmother, who had helped raise her and whom she affectionately called Granny, interjected, "Nonsense. You are fine. I don't see what the big fuss is about. It's just the three of us anyways." Granny smoothed the front of her fire engine-colored hair.

Casting Granny a quick, grateful smile, Claire took in her outfit. Her granny wore a sapphire velour tracksuit, stark white tennis shoes, and the ever-present rhinestone, gold ball necklace. She chuckled. No one would make Granny do anything she didn't want to do—Margaret Thomson didn't care what others thought about her. Why couldn't Claire be more like that?

"There's four of us dining tonight," the queen mother added.

Claire raised a brow and turned her attention to her royal grandmother. "Oh? Who is it?"

A tall, handsome older gentleman entered the room as if on command. He stood over six-foot-tall with salt and pepper sprinkled around his temples. His presence filled the room, and he strode to the table with a confident clip. Stopping behind an empty chair opposite Granny, he gave a slight bow in Claire's direction.

After a few awkward seconds of silence, Claire

jolted upright. "Oh, you're waiting for me to permit you to take your seat. I still forget I have to do that. Kind of new at this whole queen thing, you know?"

He frowned. "I can't say I do."

Wow. He's super serious. Fun. "Uh, please be seated." She gestured to the empty chair.

The man gave a stiff nod and pulled the chair back, practically floating into it. He lifted his napkin from his plate and spread it methodically across his lap as if he were making military corners on a bed.

Claire looked at her granny and mouthed the words, "Who is this guy?"

Granny shrugged and rolled her eyes, providing no help.

"Allow me to make the introduction," a low voice interjected.

Whipping around, Claire tensed her shoulders, and the blood in her veins turned cold.

Maurelle.

Claire's stepmother entered the dining room, wearing a floor-length black gown, along with her signature high heels and red nails. "Claire," she waved a manicured hand toward the stranger, "may I present Lord Edward Smythe Chicanery." She dipped her head toward her stepdaughter. "Lord Chicanery, this is my stepdaughter, Dr. Claire Thomson."

The queen mother cleared her throat. "Don't you mean, Queen Claire? Hmm? Let's not suffer a lapse in protocol. Tradition remains one of the pillars of our fine country and what strengthens us."

Maurelle's eyes narrowed. She barely sputtered her response through pursed lips, as if she might choke on the words as they shot from her mouth, "Of course. Forgive me, Queen Claire. It's so hard to adjust to your new title. Not too long ago, I carried the only title of the queen at Evercliff, so you can understand my mistake." She gave an exaggerated curtsy and lowered her head, but Claire noticed the smirk forming at the corners of Maurelle's lips as she bowed her head.

Let it go. "No problem, Maurelle. I'm not too hung up on titles."

Maurelle took a seat next to the gentleman without invitation. She slithered into her chair and tilted her head toward one of the waitstaff.

The waiter dashed to Maurelle's side, carrying a full place setting complete with a napkin and a finger bowl.

Lord Chicanery sent Claire a sidelong stare as if surveying the competition on a battlefield. "Yes, I can see that. However, I come from a long line of monarchs, and I agree with your grandmother. Titles—along with tradition, legacy, and appearance—matter."

There it was again. The importance of how things looked. Why did the world demand a filtered version of life? Claire wanted to live authentically, but fear of failing, disappointing others, and especially letting her grandmother down prohibited authenticity. She glanced at her empty plate, and suddenly her appetite vanished.

"I suppose you're right," she agreed.

Granny slapped her hand on the table, startling the entire dinner party. "I won't hear any of that—not about my granddaughter. She's a wonderful girl, a fine doctor, and in my opinion, a fantastic queen. You couldn't find anyone else better than her to do the job. I don't see why it matters what she wears or how she looks. Silly if you ask me." She emphasized her sentiments by clanging her fork on her empty water goblet to catch the attention of a staffer. It was her way of asking for a refill.

Claire snickered. She couldn't help it—it popped out. Her eyes flicked toward her grandmother. "I'm sorry. Why don't we say grace and begin dinner?"

Her grandmother nodded. "Yes, that would probably be for the best."

Claire bowed her head and waited for the queen mother to lead the dinner prayer, but the room fell silent and remained that way. She opened one eye and peered at the opposite end of the table.

Her grandmother sent her a quick flick of the head, indicating that it was Claire's job to lead the way.

Right. Another thing the queen does. "Uh, thank you, God, for today and this food. May you bless the hands that prepared it, and, um, thank you for protecting it from Wilson. Amen."

Granny chuckled and then muttered, "You got that right. How many meals has that dog ruined?"

Maurelle's powerful voice boomed from down the

table, "Seven."

"Oh, really? Huh. That many?" Claire tilted her head, considering this figure and reflecting on the memories in her mind to determine the accuracy of her stepmother's estimation.

"That many. Seven." Maurelle placed her napkin in her lap and glared at Claire.

A waiter set a plate filled with chicken, rice, salad, and a gelatinous red substance before Claire. She looked at the staffer. "Thank you." The waiter bowed at the waist and hurried away to get the pitcher of water. "Well, at least it's God's perfect number."

Granny erupted in an uncontained fit of giggles.

Claire tittered, too, and a few laughs later, water snorted from her nose.

Maurelle didn't attempt to hide her disgust this time. She turned to Lord Chicanery. "I must apologize for these antics. We do not normally behave in such a manner."

Between snickering and wiping at her eyes with a napkin, Granny sputtered, "Sure we do. We act like this all the time. If you're going to hang around with my granddaughter, you might as well get used to it."

Claire composed herself quickly. She dabbed at her nose and then glanced at the queen mother, unsure of what to do or say next. On the one hand, Claire loved her granny, and honestly, her assessment of the situation was spot-on. Nonetheless, she didn't want to make a wrong step in her first few weeks as queen, and

Claire hated to disappoint her grandmother as well as the people of Amorley. Plus, with her track record with the newspaper, who knew if this guy might talk to someone and have Claire's picture along with Granny's front page by tomorrow morning. She could envision the headline now: *Local Queen's Manners Missing—Debuts Dinner Party Trick, but No One's Laughing.*

"Sorry about that." Claire composed herself and tossed her napkin under the table. Maybe no one would notice.

"Hmm," Lord Chicanery replied, staring at her as if she'd sprouted a second head.

Claire cleared her throat. "What brings you to Evercliff? Please forgive my ignorance about your visit. No one informed me of it." She sent a pointed look toward Maurelle.

Maurelle's eyes morphed from serene to gleeful. "Oh, you don't know about Lord Chicanery, do you? He's an important man in his home country, Maltenstein." She glanced at him. "You're what—fifth in line for the throne there?"

He gave a slight nod, and his eyes darkened.

Yikes. It must be a sore subject. Note to self—avoid the topic of lineage in Maltenstein. "I see. Uh, are you here for pleasure or business?" Claire took a bite of her chicken and raised a brow.

Lord Chicanery wiped the edges of his lips with his napkin before responding, "A bit of both. I've known Maurelle since childhood, and when I learned that a new queen had risen to power in Amorley, I thought it was a good time to visit and secure relations between your country and mine while reacquainting myself with the enchanting Maurelle." He peered at Claire's stepmother, interest filling his eyes.

Huh. I bet there's a story there. Perhaps Lord Chicanery was an old flame. Claire swallowed her bite and opened her mouth. "I—"

"Were you two an item when you were younger or what?" Granny prodded in her typical, brash way.

Maurelle gasped, and her hand flew to her mouth.

Lord Chicanery, to his credit, didn't flinch, but his face paled a bit. "Well, as I said, we've known one another a long time, and I've always been fond of Maurelle. Of course, she moved away and married your father, King Alexander Evercliff, and I married as well. Sadly, my wife suffered an accident a few years ago, leaving me alone with my son, Hans."

The mention of loss tugged at Claire's heart. Although she still didn't trust Maurelle's intentions, and maybe not Lord Chicanery's either, the pain of loss felt fresh to Claire, and she empathized with the gentleman. "I'm sorry about your wife. How awful."

The man swallowed hard before answering, "Yes, well, as they say, these things happen. I loved my wife, but she understood better than anyone the duties that come with nobility. That's why she would have approved of my trip to Evercliff."

"Oh, really? Why's that?" Claire scooted a rogue

pea around her plate. She still hated them—always had since childhood. Her mother made them at least once a week and told her to eat them so she'd grow big and strong. Granny had looked the other way when Claire systematically hid each offending green orb under the other food on her plate.

Granny caught Claire's eye.

Claire shoved the few remaining peas under a pile of mashed potatoes and peeked at her granny again.

Granny sent her a wink.

Claire smiled and shrugged.

"Because she would have encouraged me to do anything in my power to better Maltenstein and my family, so that's what I'm doing today." Lord Chicanery returned his napkin to the side of his plate and straightened his posture.

Puzzled, Claire frowned. "Not that I don't want you to better your family, but I don't see what it has to do with me."

Now Maurelle's mouth curled upward, revealing a wide, toothy smile.

Uh-oh. Claire had seen that look several times before. It was never good—it meant Maurelle had a secret that wouldn't end well for her stepdaughter.

"It has everything to do with you," Lord Chicanery continued. "You see, it has come to my attention that—and forgive me for putting it this way—you may be unfit to rule."

Claire gasped. *How dare he. Unfit to rule?* Hadn't

she proven herself time and time again? Okay, she didn't have the best track record with the newspaper. Then there had been the occasional medical emergency, but honestly, she was a physician. What did the country expect? "How can you say that?" she whispered, anger coursing through her veins.

He raised a hand. "It isn't my intention to offend you, but you must be married within three months of your coronation according to the Constitution."

"I will be," Claire huffed. "We have discussed the wedding date, begun work on the dress, and the planning is underway. Things are going smoothly." Not entirely true. Mademoiselle Couture would argue this point, but Claire wouldn't let him or Maurelle know that.

He lifted a palm in her direction. "Yes, I'm simply reminding you of a rule that is the law. Not my law, mind you, but yours."

Maurelle clasped her hands together and feigned an apologetic smile. "Dear, I'm afraid that's not all."

Granny jumped from her seat. Although short in stature, she could intimidate anyone. As a child, Claire quickly learned what Granny said became law. "Afraid, my eyeball. You love stirring up things. I bet you dug up this drama and called Lord Fancypants to come here yourself. I wouldn't put it past you."

Claire placed a hand on Granny's forearm. "Let me handle this. Your heart—I don't want you upset. Remember what the doctor said at the last visit." A week ago, Claire had taken her grandmother to a follow-up appointment after she'd collapsed from third-degree heart block the day before Claire's coronation. Fortunately, the physician said that Granny had recovered, but he encouraged her to get plenty of rest, eat healthy foods, and avoid stress. So far, Claire stood zero for three on those counts.

Granny waved Claire's arm away. "Pshaw. You agreed to the heart doctor's nonsense, but I didn't go along with it. I know my body, and right now, it says its job is to defend you and make sure this—" she gestured with her thumb toward Maurelle, "sneaky, ill-mannered—"

"Granny! Please." Claire pulled in a deep breath and exhaled slowly.

Raising both palms in front of her, Granny relented. "Fine. I'll be quiet, but don't let her walk all over you." She returned to her seat and glared across the table at Maurelle.

Maurelle's eyes darkened. "I assure you my intention is not to 'walk all over' Claire but rather to ensure that the future of Amorley and its people remains bright. Lord Chicanery and his country could offer a great alliance to Amorley. His country carries great wealth and power."

Lord Chicanery spoke up, "If I may say something—"

Claire nodded for him to continue.

"I have several meetings over the coming weeks

with Parliament. I sincerely hope that our two countries might find a way to work together. My country can offer strong military protection and a firm handle on the political climate of the world. I have many friends in high places."

Claire raised a brow. "What exactly can Amorley offer you, then?"

He clasped his hands together in front of him. "In recent times, my country has struggled with some financial challenges. Not my fault or that of my family, but there you have it. If we become an ally to you and provide a strong military force, I hope your government might extend a financial incentive to us in return. There are many other ways we could help one another, too."

Claire's mouth fell open. *Was this guy serious?* He couldn't be, but there he sat, his stiff smile in place, waiting for some sort of response from her. "Um, well, I can't give you an answer on that point at this time."

"Oh, I didn't expect one from you. Technically, your Parliament would be the one to approve my request. That's why I'm here and planned meetings with them. Oh, there is one other matter."

Holding her breath, Claire caught his gaze. *What else could there be?* He'd already asked for money and a free place to stay for who knows how long. "Yes, what's that?"

"I found an interesting item in your Constitution. The funny thing about those old pieces of paper— they're filled with nuanced rules and appendices. Did you know you can't have more than five cows per five acres of land?" he asked.

"I did not know that, but is that the critical piece of information you wanted to share with me? About cows?" Claire closed her eyes, bracing herself for the proverbial shoe to drop.

He sat even straighter. Now his spine looked like someone had placed a backboard inside his shirt—the kind they used at crash scenes. If he sat any more erect, he'd probably hit the ceiling. *Relax, dude.*

"No, of course not. The cow tidbit is simply an example. My point is this—you never know what information hides in those articles and footnotes. All kinds of important stuff. For example, are you aware of the law that requires the ruler to manage Amorley's financial affairs in a modest and responsible manner?"

Claire almost snorted. Didn't this guy just ask for Amorley's financial help, and then he turns around and accuses her of mismanagement of her country's affairs? Her stomach clenched, and bile hit the back of her mouth. *Not again. Not another hurdle to jump.* She turned to her stepmother. "How many more of these little 'rules' can you find, Maurelle?"

Maurelle put her hand to her chest, her mouth forming a small circle. "Who me? I didn't know anything about this. I'd heard that Lord Chicanery was planning a visit, but I knew nothing of this wedding rule. Although, I can't imagine it will be a problem for you. Aren't you to be married within the three months' timeframe? Don't you believe you can handle Amorley's economics? What could go wrong?"

What could go wrong? Claire could think of many things, most of them instigated by Maurelle. "I'm sure you're right." She wasn't sure at all, but Claire refused to let Maurelle or Lord Chicanery see her sweat. Instead, she folded her napkin, set it next to her plate, and placed her fork at the bottom of the dish, indicating the meal had concluded.

Claire rose from her seat and nodded at Lord Chicanery. "Welcome to Evercliff. I hope you have a good evening. Albert will see you to your room. Now, if you'll excuse me—I have many items to attend to early in the morning but enjoy your time at the castle."

Everyone at the table stood and waited as Claire left the room.

She heard the clinking of glasses and dishes as the waiters cleared them away. Chairs scraped against the floor as the dinner guests readied themselves to leave.

Sighing, Claire took each stair up the grand staircase slowly. Three months. Sure, they'd discussed having the wedding soon, but the reality of planning and executing her dream wedding in such a short timeframe caused her heart to beat faster. Add in the many public appearances and her hospital job to the mix, and she didn't know how she'd manage it all. Oh, and she had to prove to everyone that she could run the country effectively while acting and looking perfect.

Claire couldn't let her late father down and

disgrace his legacy. She wouldn't. Pulling back her shoulders, Claire headed to her bedroom. She opened the door and shut it behind her with the force of her resolve to prove Maurelle, Lord Chicanery, and her own doubts wrong.

Chapter 3

"What do you mean you want to elope?" Ethan's eyes widened as the words tumbled from his lips.

"I'm not saying that's what we should do, only that it's a consideration." Claire refused to meet his eyes. Instead, she bent down to pick up a stick from the ground. She mindlessly scraped circular shapes across the pebbled path behind the castle.

Ethan had arrived at the front door early and surprised her with her favorite treat—doughnuts and coffee—and not some fancy, stuffy version of a doughnut but the real deal.

After wrestling with her sheets all night, she'd barely kept her eyes open during her morning consultation with Albert and her assistant about the day's plans.

Even though the castle made coffee for her daily, it paled in comparison to what she'd become accustomed to back home in Boston. When Ethan arrived, coffee travel cup in hand, Claire flung her arms around his neck with such force that he'd nearly dropped her beloved drink.

After inviting him inside long enough to suck down her beverage and obtain an appropriate caffeine rush, he had suggested they take a morning stroll through the castle's gardens.

"Why would we elope? We're planning a wedding—a big wedding. In case it has slipped your mind, you are the queen of a country, and the queen mother will not be pleased if her sole granddaughter and the ruler of her country runs off to Las Vegas to get married. Not to mention the media frenzy such a move would create."

Claire tossed the stick into the bushes. "I never said we'd go to Vegas. I thought a quiet beach sounded nice. Besides, I don't know if I'm cut out for this ruler business. Maybe we should get married and move back to Boston. I could apply for a job at the hospital there or even teach at the medical school. You could run your own financial consulting business, or you could teach. We could both be teachers. Doesn't that sound wonderful? Imagine the two of us out of the spotlight, living a quiet life in a brownstone in Boston. Granny and Wilson could come with us. Then Maurelle, her son, Eric, or maybe even Lord Chicanery could have the throne."

Ethan's jaw dropped. He stopped walking and crossed his arms over his broad chest. His blond hair glistened in the sunlight, contrasting handsomely with the sapphire color of his eyes. "Claire, I love you."

She sent him a half-smile. "I love you, too."

"And because I love you, I will be honest. You are scared. We've been through all of this before. Remember? You didn't think you could take the throne in the first place. Maurelle's tried to steal your power time and time again, but God's given you the favor and grace to rule. Don't give up now. Don't run. It would make you miserable."

She wasn't convinced. How inviting a beach wedding with a few guests sounded.

He must have noticed her reluctance. "Think of it. Once you returned home and the dust settled, you'd regret letting fear win—letting Maurelle win. Come on. Let's fight. Let's fight for what's right. I know you're afraid of failing, of what people think, of not meeting everyone's expectations, but I'm telling you the truth— you can do this. I love you. Granny loves you. We will be here with you every step of the way." He closed the gap between them and rested his hands on her shoulders.

She lifted her face toward his and searched his eyes. "You really think I can do this?"

Ethan stared at her with intensity, his brows furrowed. "I do." He caressed his thumb across her cheek and tilted her chin to brush his lips against hers.

Claire's heart pounded.

He framed her cheek and kissed her with urgency.

She couldn't wait to marry this man. As Claire melted into him, her shoulders relaxed. Reluctantly, she pulled away and stared deeply into his eyes.

Ethan smiled. "Don't worry about Maurelle and Lord Chicanery. We've faced threats from your stepmother before, and you've overcome them."

Claire drew in a deep breath and released it, considering the past. "I hope you're right."

"I know I am," Ethan kissed her forehead. "Let's focus on the wedding. What can I do to help?"

She trailed her finger down his cheek and frowned. "Ugh. The wedding."

He raised both hands in the air, palms facing forward. "Hey, don't sound so excited." Ethan chuckled.

Claire shook her head, causing her blonde locks to sway from side to side. "It's not that I don't want to marry you—I do. Of course, I do. It's everything we have to do before the wedding day. Not only do we have to finalize attire, but we must also select a dinner menu, invitations, and who knows what else. Plus, I have a million other public appearances to do before then. For starters, there is a high tea tomorrow afternoon."

"Why are you so worried about the public appearances? You've done a great job so far." Ethan rubbed her shoulders with his hands.

Claire snorted. "Yeah, a great job. I botched a polo match, mangled several hospital-related events, and I almost forgot my entire speech for my coronation."

Ethan grabbed her hand. "Come with me. I want to

show you something." Leading her further down the pebbled path, they passed several still-flowering magnolia trees toward the edge of the gardens. The bushes parted and revealed the still-watered lake. "Have a seat." He nodded to the grassy patch next to him.

She sank to the ground, careful to tuck her skirt underneath her. Staring at the tranquil water, she inhaled and exhaled slowly. "I always forget how beautiful it is here."

Ethan took a spot next to her and leaned back, resting on his hands. He closed his eyes and let the sun warm his face. "We never take time to remind ourselves of its beauty. That's why I brought you. I wanted to remind you of the beauty within you. It doesn't matter how you give a speech, what outfit you wear, or what the newspapers say. Why? Because you're beautiful on the inside and outside. Perfection isn't what makes you beautiful. God's love lives inside of you—that's what makes you beautiful." He opened one eye at Claire.

Her cheeks warmed, and she sent him a smile. "Thanks, Ethan. I love you."

"I love you, too."

Claire closed her eyes and tossed her hair back. "Let's not discuss any wedding plans right now. Today is for us and this—you and me sitting here being in love. We'll tackle all the plans tomorrow."

Ethan scooted closer and draped an arm across her shoulder. "That sounds wonderful." Then, he leaned in and pressed his lips against hers once more.

Gratitude and hope filled Claire's heart. Nothing could stand in their way—not Maurelle, Lord Chicanery, or anyone else. Still, there was Ethan's family. He'd repaired his relationship with his parents after he saved his family's business and estate. Though he and his brother, Richard, might never be best friends, he'd left Ethan alone for the most part. In three months, Ethan would marry Claire, no matter what else happened. *Right*?

Chapter 4

Claire tried to scratch her neck discreetly under the frilly lace trim on her dress. She couldn't breathe. *Did it have starch in it? Why did it itch so much?*

"Dear, please try to sit still. Lord Chicanery will be here any moment," the queen mother admonished.

Even though Claire technically ruled now, she still wanted to please her grandmother.

Granny snorted. "Who could sit still in that contraption? Look at her. She looks more like a mummy than a queen. Why, I've seen toilet-paper gowns at bridal showers that looked more comfortable than that dress."

Claire's cheeks warmed. "Granny, you can't say things like that." She glanced at the queen mother. "It's a lovely dress." *Except it looks like it's five hundred years old and feels that way, too.*

The queen mother gave a small smile and pushed her wire-rim glasses higher on her nose. Her assistant had crafted her hair into a helmet shape that glistened with a high sheen from an entire can of spray. Her grandmother's outfit consisted of a matching tweed, embroidered navy suit and skirt.

Claire narrowed her eyes at her grandmother's attire. *It must be a hundred degrees in that thing. How can she stand it?* She dug at her neck again, this time without discretion.

The queen mother frowned. "Claire, stop scratching."

"I'm trying, but the lace is irritating my neck." This dress—her great, great, great, oh, who knows how many greats—grandmother's gown had miraculously but unfortunately fit her. The outfit had produced snickers when she'd put it on earlier and showed it to her granny. Even now, when Claire let her eyes land on Granny's face, she saw a teasing glint in her eyes. "Thanks," she mouthed.

Granny shrugged and began whistling show tunes.

As Claire smoothed out the skirt of her dress and shifted in her seat, Lord Chicanery and another gentleman who appeared much younger than him entered the room. She flicked her eyes toward the duo and pasted a smile on her face. "Lord Chicanery, how delightful of you to join us for tea," she spoke in the clear, smooth voice her grandmother had practiced with her during their royal lessons.

Wearing a charcoal suit and tie, Chicanery dipped his head and took a seat at the table across from the queen mother and Claire's granny. "Thank you for having me." He gestured toward the younger man who stood next to him. "This is my son, Hans."

Hans bent slightly at the waist in Claire's direction before taking a seat next to his father. "How do you do?" He smiled, revealing a dimple in his cheek, and his aqua eyes glinted with a hint of mischief. His blond hair was cut short and gelled back, and he wore a clean shave.

If hard-pressed, Claire had to admit he looked like a movie star—not that she noticed. She loved Ethan with all her heart, but she conceded the man was handsome in a purely observational moment. She pasted on another smile. "I'm well. Thank you. I didn't realize that you'd be joining your father here at Evercliff. If he mentioned it the last time we spoke, then I must have forgotten." Her eyes flicked toward Lord Chicanery. How many more mystery people would show up this week?

Hans glanced at his father. "You didn't tell me that the queen of Amorley was so beautiful. Of course, I've seen photographs of you in newspaper articles, but I must say, they do not do you justice. You're stunning."

Claire's cheeks burned. She stammered, "Thank you."

Lord Chicanery gave her a paper-thin smile. "I apologize. I didn't hear from Hans until yesterday about his plans. He was supposed to be on a foreign-relations trip in America, but it was postponed. I hope your fiancé won't mind that we are here in the middle of your wedding-planning season."

Hans's grin widened. "Yes, I hope your fiancé won't mind that I'm staying here. If you were my bride-to-be, I wouldn't want any other man underfoot."

Claire's tongue wouldn't cooperate in formulating a response, so she stalled by taking a long sip of water. After having a moment to think, she placed the glass down. "My fiancé trusts me. Although, he might not appreciate the flattery." She lifted her chin and stared him down. Hopefully, he'd get the message and back off.

Instead, he sent her a subtle wink while everyone else at the table chatted. "What is his name, this fiancé of yours?"

She glared. "His name is Ethan. Ethan Kane, Earl of Abbingdon."

Footsteps echoed from the hallway, and Ethan's familiar voice broke the tension, "I thought I heard my name. Sorry that I'm late." He walked to the table with confident steps and took the empty seat next to the head of the table where Claire sat, then reached for her hand and squeezed it.

Claire peered at her fiancé, and her cheeks warmed. "Oh, we were just discussing the wedding plans."

Hans cleared his throat. "I told Claire what a blessed man Ethan Kane must be to have landed such a talented and beautiful woman—and a queen, no less." He flashed a wide grin in Claire's direction.

Her eyes darted between Ethan and Hans, watching

the subtle yet palpable, silent interchange between the two men. They might as well have been pounding their chests like cave dwellers.

She saw Ethan's jaw clench before he responded. "I am a blessed man, and I know it. As I'm sure you are discovering, Claire is an intelligent, kind, and gorgeous woman, and in a few months, I will have the honor of making her my bride."

Hans cocked his head to the side and looked at the couple. "Of course, well, I had read somewhere that the wedding was happening soon. I'm sure you want to get things underway before she has a chance to change her mind." His eyes darted to Claire's, and he sent her another wink. "Plus, you don't want to give someone else a chance to swoop in and steal her away."

Claire's heart pounded. She could only imagine what thoughts raced through Ethan's mind. After a few seconds of awkward silence, she didn't have to guess.

"Yes, well, I guarantee that won't happen. I love Claire, and she loves me, and nothing will stand in the way of our wedding or our love." His eyes were cold enough to freeze the air between him and Hans. "Nothing," he enunciated.

Hans lifted his palms. "I'm sure you're right. Still—things happen." With this final thought, the handsome interloper turned his attention to a conversation underway between his father and the queen mother.

Ethan leaned over and whispered in Claire's ear, "I

don't trust that guy—not at all."

Claire hissed back, "Neither do I, but what can I do? They are here as Maurelle's guests. I suppose I could kick them out of the castle but imagine the public-relations nightmare that would create. Can't you picture the tabloids?" She raised her brow.

At that moment, one of the waitstaff appeared at Claire's side and placed a plate before her filled with scones, fruit, cream, and lemon curd. Another staffer filled an empty cup with hot tea and then moved on to the next guest. Within minutes the waiters had served everyone at the table.

The guests turned their attention to Claire, awaiting her commencement of the meal.

"I want to thank everyone in advance for their support of mine and Ethan's upcoming marriage. We cannot wait to begin a new chapter of our lives together. I'd like to offer a toast to my fiancé." She reached for her crystal water glass, ready to lift it high, feeling quite proud of how she'd handled an uncomfortable situation. As her arm extended forward, Maurelle sneezed, and the sound startled Claire. Her hand jerked, knocking her glass into the nearest candlestick—which was lit. It toppled like a game of dominos and landed flame side down on the linen tablecloth.

The tablecloth erupted in flames. Within ten seconds, the meal went from subtle, unspoken threats to a full-out blazing inferno.

"Ah! Call for help. Fire!" Claire's grandmother screamed toward the kitchen for assistance.

The chef flew into the dining room, and his eyes popped wide. "Wha—What in the world happened? The table's on fire."

Claire jumped up, grabbed the closest water goblet to her, and tossed it at the flames.

The dancing sparks fizzled, teasing her briefly, but then resurged with greater force.

Ethan's eyes widened. "We need' do something."

Right. Do something. After all, she was the queen, and she wouldn't let her first year in the castle go up in flames. *Literally.* Claire glanced around the table, looking for help, but all she found were more piddly water glasses. "Wait here. I'll see if there's a fire extinguisher in the kitchen."

Before Ethan could respond, Claire dashed off toward the kitchen. She nearly plowed over Albert.

"Your Majesty, what's wrong?" His forehead creased.

"Help. The table's on fire. Quick. I need something to put it out. Is there a fire extinguisher? I can't burn down my father's castle." She wrung her hands and scanned the room. Her eyes landed on a large vessel filled with water. "Aha. The pot. That will do." Claire heaved it into her arms and ran out of the kitchen with Albert on her heels.

"Your Majesty, you can't use that. It—"

"No time for conversation right now, Albert. This

will have to do." Claire made a beeline for the dining table and flung the entire contents of the pot onto the flames.

For a brief moment, the flames diminished and looked like they would subside. After a few seconds, a loud whooshing sound filled the room, followed by a vindictive resurgence in the blaze. The red tendrils leaped twice as tall and spread to both ends of the table, engulfing it.

Albert sped to her side. "I tried to warn you. That pot contained cooking grease. You tossed fuel on the fire."

Claire's knees weakened, and her knees buckled.

Ethan grabbed her arm and tugged her away from the table. "You can't do anything more right now. We must evacuate. It's not safe."

Bile rose and filled the back of her throat. Now she'd done it—she'd caught Evercliff Castle on fire—a structure that had stood for hundreds of years and boasted many lifetimes of stories in its wooden halls. Now, she'd probably burned it to the ground. "I can't leave. We've got to save the castle."

Ethan dashed from her side to assist the queen mother and Granny, helping them out of their seats and guiding them toward Claire. He flung protective arms around all three women and ushered them out of the dining room, down the hallway, and through the front door to safety.

Fresh air blasted Claire's face, and she gulped it

greedily. Stumbling down the stairs, she sank to the ground.

Granny made her way over to her granddaughter and eased herself down next to Claire. "Well, when you do it, you do it. Talk about a way to avoid an uncomfortable meal."

Claire glanced at her granny. "It was an accident. I bumped into the candlestick with my glass. I still don't know how I…I can't believe…there are no words."

"I have some." Maurelle marched toward Claire with arms crossed in front of her chest, her nostrils flared. With Claire sitting on the ground, she towered over her like a dragon, ready to emit her own set of flames from her nose.

Claire rubbed her arms, shivering despite the warm summer afternoon. "Maurelle, I didn't mean to—It was an accident."

"Oh, I'm sure it was. Everything with you is an accident. Your entire reign is an accident. How many things will you have to destroy before you realize this isn't where you belong? Now, you might have destroyed your father's legacy for good. Did I hear Albert say you tossed cooking grease on the fire? Every simpleton knows that grease feeds flames. Honestly, didn't your mother teach you anything?"

Granny tensed next to Claire. "Now, listen here, missy, I don't know who you think you are, but my granddaughter has done nothing wrong. I don't ever want to hear my daughter's name tumble out of that mouth of yours again. Everyone makes mistakes, and my granddaughter's the best thing that's happened to this country since—"

A fire engine siren sounded in the distance, growing louder with its wailing as it approached.

Claire exhaled a sigh of relief. "Look, help is here. Maybe it won't be too bad." *Maybe.*

Maurelle snorted. "Yes. Perhaps the whole place won't disintegrate into cinders." Then, she spun on her heel and stormed away.

"Good riddance," Granny muttered.

"She's not wrong, you know. This is one hundred percent my fault. I may have ruined my father's home and generations' worth of history because I'm a klutz." Claire's eyes filled with tears.

Granny wrapped an arm around Claire. "Nonsense. There's nothing too big for God to fix, including this. Those firefighters will put the flames out, and then we'll see what needs repairing. I bet by the end of the week; everything will be as good as new."

Claire sent her granny a small smile. "I hope you're right."

One fireman emerged from the castle's front door and removed his helmet. He ran a hand through his hair and scanned the crowd. Once his gaze fell upon Claire, recognition crossed his face. His mouth settled into a grim line, and he walked toward her.

She pressed her hands against her thighs to stand and brushed off debris from her skirt. Extending a hand to the fireman, she introduced herself, "I'm Dr. Claire Thomson."

He didn't take her hand as it wasn't customary to shake the queen's hand. Claire kept forgetting that. Instead, he bowed at the waist. "Your Majesty. It's an honor to meet you, albeit under such unfortunate circumstances."

"Yes. Of course. What can you tell me about the castle? Is it bad?" She clenched her hands together, hoping he'd deliver good news.

The man frowned and ran his hand through his hair again. "It's not good. The fire remained confined to the dining room, but some smoke damage exists through the main hallway, too. The fire destroyed the dining room table."

Claire sighed. "Oh, well, that doesn't sound terrible. So, we just need to replace a table and air out the hallway? That's not bad."

The queen mother appeared at Claire's side. She'd heard the interchange between her granddaughter and the fireman. "That table, young lady, is over two hundred years old. It belonged to your father's family, and we cannot replace it."

Claire's hand flew to her mouth. "I'm so sorry, Grandmother. I feel awful." She turned to the fireman again. "How long do you think it will take before we can use the dining room and open the hallway again?"

Lines appeared on his forehead. "I'd say at least two weeks. You will have to repaint the hallway and dining room if you want to remove the smoke smell."

"Is it okay for us to stay in the castle? As long as we don't use the affected areas until they are fixed?" Claire asked.

The fireman scratched his head. "Yes, ma'am, but don't you have the Royal Engagement Dinner next week?"

Claire's throat tightened. She'd forgotten about that. Every major dignitary, high-profile politician, and Amorley noble would be attending. It would function as a pre-wedding celebration, and she could not postpone it. "Right. I forgot about that." She peered at the firefighter, noting the deep lines on his forehead, the wrinkles around his eyes, and his tanned skin. Claire guessed his age approximated her father's. "Wait. How do you know about the dinner?"

He smiled, and his eyes crinkled even more. "Why? Does it surprise you that a burly fireman would know about high society?"

Claire's face burned, and this time it wasn't from the heat of the flames. "No—no, that's not what I meant. I only asked because...I didn't mean to offend you...It's just—"

He chuckled and raised a hand. "Don't worry. I'm not offended. My wife is obsessed with the royal family. She reads the tabloids and newspapers every day and keeps me in the know."

A flash popped, causing Claire to jump. She turned and saw it was a photographer who worked for the firehouse documenting the scene.

The fireman lifted his hand to his forehead, shielding his eyes. "Speaking of the tabloids, the paparazzi will probably arrive soon. Guess this will be in the morning paper."

"No," Claire whispered. *Not again.* Why did this keep happening to her? Why couldn't she get things right?

The fireman noticed the change in her demeanor and sent her a kind smile. "Hey, don't worry about it. Most people don't even read the newspaper."

"Right." Claire doubted the queen mother would see it that way, and even though she'd hoped once she'd taken the throne, it wouldn't matter what others thought of her, she'd quickly discovered it mattered even more. Everyone judged everything she said, did, and thought. If Claire had to guess what the court of public opinion would think about this latest debacle, she'd say the verdict would return as guilty, and the headline would read—Queen Claire isn't setting the country on fire, just her castle.

Claire raised a brow. "What about the rest of the castle? The ballroom is right next to the dining room, and we are supposed to have several parties in the coming weeks in preparation for our wedding, not to mention that our wedding reception is to be held there."

The fireman rubbed a soot-covered hand across his forehead. "I don't know what to tell you, except I doubt any of that is going to happen, at least not here. If I were you, I'd find another venue."

Claire's mouth went dry. "I can't find another venue. Every Evercliff that's gotten married has had their wedding reception in that ballroom. If we don't have it here, I'll have ruined hundreds of years of tradition."

Maurelle slithered closer and inclined her head to Claire's ear. "Perhaps you should just call off the wedding, at least for now. It doesn't sound like the reception will happen, and I can only imagine the field day the press will have over this. Perhaps you should consider postponing your wedding. Of course, there's that sticky matter about how the queen of Amorley must get married within three months or her coronation is null and void." She made a tsking sound. "Such a pity. All of your plans have gone up in flames, literally. Well, these things cannot always be helped. Perhaps, it's for the best. I'm sure that any of the other eligible family members will be ready to step forward and take your place, should your coronation face a challenge." Maurelle's hand flew to her lips. "Oh, my, that was insensitive of me, wasn't it? I apologize." Then, she smirked with a shrug of her shoulders.

Claire swallowed hard. "What could challenge my coronation? I already went through a coronation. You were there, Ethan was there, everyone was there. It happened."

Maurelle's lips pulled into a tight smile. "Yes, but remember, the Constitution clearly states that if the current monarch isn't crowned and married within three months, then the coronation, and therefore that individual's appointment to the throne is null and void." She tapped a red fingernail on her chin. "Finito."

Claire narrowed her eyes. Before she could formulate a rebuttal, her stepmother spun around and sauntered away.

"Ooh, that woman makes me so mad." Claire clenched her fists at her side.

"Yes, well, I can see why. Not the most pleasant person, but as I was saying, you're going to be able to reenter the castle tonight to use the bedrooms, but you must avoid the dining room, main hallway, and the ballroom." The fireman pulled out a clipboard and scribbled on a stack of papers.

Claire leaned forward, peering at the documents. "What are you writing?"

The man didn't meet her gaze but remained focused on his work. "Oh, I have to write up the incident. My report includes the preliminarily cause of the fire and how we left the residence. Standard operating procedure."

Claire chewed on the inside of her mouth. "Uh, those forms—they don't happen to be part of public record, do they?"

The fireman continued writing. "Yes. Every emergency call that isn't medically related goes into the public record. Besides, the press won't need my forms to discover what's happening. They usually listen to the scanners and send reporters out on calls."

Claire jerked upright. "I didn't say anything about the press, but I—"

He stopped writing and met her gaze. His eyes softened. "I overheard you mention something about the press having a field day. You should prepare yourself—they are on the way. They usually aren't far behind us when we head out on celebrity calls. You might want to duck inside or head around back."

Claire's heartbeat quickened. "Right. Thanks for the warning." She hurried over to Ethan, who stood beside her granny, to warn him. "We need to head to the garden. The fireman said that—"

Ethan interrupted her, "The press is coming."

Claire stared at her fiancé. "Right. Exactly. How did you know that's what he said?"

He tilted his head behind Claire. "Because the press *is* coming."

Claire spun around in time to see three large white vans whip into the driveway, each with a different news station's emblem painted across the side of the vehicle.

So much for security…and saving face. Claire grabbed Ethan's and Granny's arms. "Come on. We have to go." She managed to flee before the news frenzy erupted, but not before one bright flash from a photographer's camera nearly blinded her eyes. "Great. Just perfect."

Claire ducked her head and stared at the ground as she made her way to safety. "Whatever it takes, I'm getting married as planned, and I'm having my reception here, just like my father and every other Evercliff before him have done. I don't care what Maurelle says—I'm not letting her or anyone else takes away my birthright."

Granny clucked her tongue. "That's the spirit. Now, what are we going to do about dinner since you burned ours up?"

Chapter 5

Ethan lowered his head and focused on the little white orb below him. He drew in a deep breath and took a swing at the ball. The satisfying whack released some of his frustration and anxiety, at least for a moment. He lifted his head and followed the golf ball as it flew through the air. "It's going to fall short."

"What does Father always say?" Richard sidled up and rested his hand on his golf club.

Sighing, Ethan repeated the mantra he'd heard his father repeat many times, "You must try. You didn't even try. If you're going to aim for something, always shoot beyond the mark. If you fall short, you'll never make it."

Richard chuckled. "Exactly. You always hit short. You've got to go for it." He slapped his brother's shoulder and took his place behind his ball, ready for his turn. After preparing his stance and drawing his arms back, he produced a second loud crack, and the two brothers watched Richard's ball arc in the sky. In contrast to Ethan's attempt, Richard's swing proved more successful.

Ethan shifted his weight. "It's going to be long."

Richard grinned and caught Ethan's gaze. "Yeah, but at least I made it past my goal. Aim long, my friend. Aim long."

Ethan smirked. "Thanks for the advice."

Reaching down to pull his golf tee from the ground, Richard grunted, "Did you talk to Claire about our father's plans for the family business?"

"That he wants to take it global? That he wants to expand our real estate holdings not only beyond Amorley's boundaries but to the United States and the rest of Europe? No, it didn't come up as the million-year-old table erupted in flames during tea. We were too busy fleeing the castle to discuss finances and real estate." Ethan hung his head and tapped his gold club against the ground. Ever since he and his family had reconciled, he had made an effort to spend at least one day a week with his brother. It was refreshing not to bicker all the time, but that didn't mean Richard would cease ribbing him.

Richard shrugged. "I guess you're right. Still, you will have to tell her about Father's ideas—and soon. The wedding is only months away, right? Unless the two of you have decided to postpone it. I imagine if the wedding venue burned up, then that might delay your plans."

Not wanting to talk about the wedding, fire, or family business, Ethan tipped his head in the direction of the green. "Come on. Let's finish this round. I want to see how badly I'm going to beat you today—even if I fell short a few times."

Richard laughed. "You wish. I'm winning this time, big brother."

The two men walked together in silence, closing the gap between themselves and the putting green. Ethan couldn't help but feel that as the distance between himself and the chance to win this game closed, so did the time he had left to right all the wrongs in his life—the wedding, the family business, the constant threat to his and Claire's happiness.

Maurelle would likely not stop until she'd burned down everything in her path. He didn't know how Maurelle planned to take over the throne by ruining their wedding or Claire's good standing before Parliament, but he didn't doubt she had something up her satin sleeve.

~

Granny bit into an apple, the juice from the fruit trickling down her chin. "You've got a little something there." Claire winked at Ethan, who sat next to her on the red-checkered blanket, handed her granny a clean napkin, and then pointed at her blouse.

Staring off into the distance, Granny didn't respond for a second. "Huh?" She turned her attention to Claire and the cloth in front of her. "Oh, I'm a mess, aren't I?"

Claire laughed. "You are, but I still love you." She

handed Ethan a glass of iced tea as he munched on a sandwich. Something must have happened at his golf game. Ever since his arrival, he'd worn a permanent furrow on his brow.

Ethan's frown deepened. "I hate to say it, but I think Maurelle's planning something. Maybe Hans and his father, too. Every time we've faced trouble, she's been in the middle of the chaos."

Moving closer to her fiancé, Claire peered around and lowered her voice, "I can't say I don't agree, but until we have proof of something underhanded going on, let's focus on what we can control—planning the perfect wedding."

Ethan finally cracked a grin. "The perfect wedding will be the one where I'm married to you at the end of it. The rest of the stuff doesn't matter."

She patted his hand. "No, you're right. Still, I'd like to make a good impression for the first major royal event since my coronation. According to Mademoiselle Couture, the entire world will be watching to see if even a strand of hair is out of place. I can't leave room for mishaps this time. Simply put, I have to be perfect."

Squeezing her hand, Ethan stared deeply into her eyes. "No one's perfect, but you're perfect for me. Don't put too much pressure on yourself."

"I won't," Claire sighed.

"Yoo-hoo." Granny waved. "Don't mind me. Please carry on with the mushy romantic talk. I'll just keep eating my apple in silence."

Claire chuckled. "Sorry, Granny. Of course, we didn't forget about you—no one could."

Granny gave Claire a playful swat on the hand. "Hush." The pleased grin on her face told Claire that her granny appreciated the compliment, despite the teasing.

Ethan broke into a story about his golf game with Richard, and Granny listened, looking happy to have his attention.

Claire drifted away from their conversation. She envisioned her perfect wedding with nothing out of place—roses and hydrangeas arranged in tall vases, silver polished to a brilliant sheen, and a gown that she hadn't tripped in or let her dog use as a wrestling mat. No, this time, things would be different. *She* would be different. *She* would be the perfect queen—even if it killed her.

Chapter 6

As Claire entered the front doors of the hospital, she exhaled. Finally, she was back where she belonged—practicing medicine. In all the whirlwind of royal activity, she hadn't felt like herself lately. Nothing fixed that quicker than setting a bone or rounding on a patient or two. She walked through the lobby and tossed a wave at a nurse she'd worked with many times.

The nurse shot back a quizzical look.

Did she have food on her face? Did something get stuck in her teeth after lunch? She slowed her steps, and the head of security, John Rogers, joined her. Ah, yes. Claire's entourage of security detail trailed behind her far enough that she almost had forgotten they were there.

She turned to face him. "Is something wrong? That nurse looked at me like I'd grown multiple heads."

He cleared his throat. "Um, ma'am, I believe your wave perplexed her."

She scrunched her forehead. "My wave? What's wrong with the way I waved?"

His face flushed red. "Nothing, except you didn't do the royal wave that the queen mother taught you. You did that American wave of yours. No disrespect." He gave a slight bow.

Claire's cheeks warmed. "Oh, right. Royal wave. Got it." How was she ever going to remember everything? Even after all these months of training and then navigating a coronation, she still couldn't get it right.

John fell back into line.

Claire continued to the elevators and pushed the button. If she could make it upstairs to her patients, then she'd feel better. Helping others was the one thing that always set her world right. Today she had a little girl to visit on whom she had performed a closed reduction of a forearm fracture yesterday and a pleasant young man who'd torn his ACL while playing soccer—or football, as they called it in Amorley. She'd never get used to that, either. Claire smiled at the thought.

The elevator door parted, and she stepped on, riding with her security team to the top floor of the hospital. When the doors opened, she adjusted her white coat and strode with the confidence it instilled in her down the hallway to see her first patient. This was her world. At the little girl's door, Claire knocked and waited.

"Come in," a female voice called from inside.

Claire glanced over her shoulder at her entourage. "Do you mind waiting here? I promise I won't sneak out the window. It's not patient privacy-compliant to have an entire SWAT team join me for the physical exam."

John nodded and took a step back.

His entire group clothed in black suits obliged and stood at ease—or as at ease as possible. They always appeared a little uptight to Claire.

She opened the door, a smile spreading naturally across her face. "Good morning. How's my favorite patient today?"

The seven-year-old blonde girl smiled from her bed. "Great. I get to meet a real princess today."

"Jenny," her mother warned, "I told you she's not a princess—she's the queen of Amorley—and you weren't to bring that up. Dr. Thomson is here as your doctor." Dark circles framed the mother's eyes. She turned to address Claire, "I apologize. I'm sure you hear this all the time. Thank you for taking a moment out of your busy schedule to see my Jenny."

Claire's cheeks warmed. "It's not a problem at all. I'm happy to do it. More and more, I'm tied up with royal obligations, so I enjoy the opportunity to take care of patients." She took a few steps closer to Jenny's bedside. "How's that arm doing?" She pointed at Jenny's casted forearm.

The little girl's eyes lit up. "Great, except it itches a little—well, a lot. Hey, would you sign my cast?" Her eyes widened.

Claire grinned. "Sure, I'd be honored."

The girl jutted a hot pink marker toward Claire with her good arm. "Put 'To Jenny, my best patient.'"

"Jenny," her mother hissed.

Claire chuckled. "It's fine. I love it." She leaned closer to the little girl's ear and whispered, "It's true, too, but don't spread it around the hospital because my other patients might get upset. Deal?" She straightened and held the marker in the air, poised to sign the girl's arm.

The girl's mouth spread into a wide smile revealing two missing front teeth. "Deal." She moved her arm closer to Claire and waited.

A few minutes later, Claire had signed Jenny's cast and discussed the post-op plan of care with the girl's mother. Once she had answered the mother's questions and listened to the little girl's third story about her dog, Claire waved goodbye and headed out the door. *Best feeling ever.*

A sudden commotion erupted in the hallway, and the security team formed a semicircle around Claire. The flash from a camera phone nearly blinded her, and she rubbed her eyes for a few seconds before opening them. *What in the world?* As her eyes parted, they landed on a gentleman whom she'd seen following her around town over the past few months. Her head of security had informed her that he belonged to an online tabloid. *How had he managed to weasel his way into the hospital past its security as well as hers?*

"Mrs. Dr. Queen Claire. You can have this." The

little girl popped out of her room and shoved the fuchsia marker in Claire's face. When Jenny noticed the gentleman taking pictures, the little girl went into full-on ham mode. "Hey, Mister, look at my cast. My doctor signed it. She says I'm her favorite patient. Want to see?" Jenny shoved her casted forearm closer to the intruder, and he grinned before snapping another blinding photo.

Claire shielded her eyes from the glaring flash, then smoothed her hair in place. Why did the press always show up when she wasn't at her best? She winced and opened one eye, peering at her semi-rumpled scrubs and plastic clog-type shoes. Okay, maybe not even close to her best—but still, why? She should be used to the idea that the media could pop up anywhere, anytime, but the concept hadn't fully settled in her mind. It probably didn't look great that she'd shown favoritism to a patient—no matter how cute the kid was.

Thankfully, Claire's head of security came to her rescue. He shoved a hand toward the photographer, half-blocking her and the girl. "Ladies and gentlemen, please take a step back and respect the privacy of the patients." John Rogers posed a daunting figure, standing at over six-foot tall and packing more than two hundred pounds of muscle. He didn't have to make his statement twice.

The media frenzy thinned out, and after a few minutes, Claire found herself alone with her security team and the little girl. Bending to one knee, Claire reached for the marker. "Thanks."

The little girl grinned and nodded, handing over the pen.

Claire smiled and stood to head down the hallway to check on another patient when her phone rang. Reaching into her white coat pocket, Claire froze upon reading the name flashing across the screen. The queen mother. Uh-oh. She hadn't told her she was heading to the hospital today because her grandmother still didn't entirely approve of anything that obstructed Claire's attention to Amorley and the throne. Had Claire missed a meeting? Has she forgotten some royal obligation? Only one way to find out—she pushed the green button. "Hello, Grandmother."

"Claire, why has Albert received three phone calls in the last five minutes concerning your fitness for the throne? One reporter mentioned that you looked like you'd been caught in a windstorm and that you were coloring with markers. Parliament is meeting in a few hours to discuss the State of the Country, and I expect you to be there on time and look presentable. Should I worry?"

Swallowing hard, Claire shook her head, even though her grandmother couldn't see her. "I'll be there on time and presentable, I promise. I can't imagine what the media printed so quickly, but I do not look like I've been in a windstorm." Her eyes drifted upward to her reflection in a walkway window. Her hair had frizzed and loosened from its ponytail, and her scrubs looked even more pummeled. "However, I wasn't coloring or doing anything frivolous or unroyal—I saw a patient, a little girl."

Her grandmother sighed. "Claire, please stay focused. You do not have time for distractions. I know how important medicine is to you, and we've discussed this before, but right now, the country needs you. Not to mention I don't trust your stepmother. Today, she invited Hans and his father to the State of the Country address. I don't know what she has planned, but I'm sure there's an ulterior motive."

Claire snorted. "I'm surprised to hear you talk about her like this—I thought you were all about giving everyone the benefit of the doubt."

"Dear, don't snort. It's not becoming of a queen. And yes, in general, I believe in looking for the best in others, but when it comes to Maurelle, well, she doesn't have the best record, does she?"

Claire grimaced at herself in the window. "No, she doesn't. Good point. Okay, I'll arrive on time, and I'll fix my hair."

Her grandmother's voice thinned, "You won't come in scrubs, will you?"

"No, of course not. I'm not completely hopeless."

The queen mother exhaled. "Good. I'll see you later. Goodbye."

"I love—" The phone clicked, and Claire met silence. "You." Sometimes she wondered if her grandmother only loved her when she did everything perfectly.

"Ma'am," the head of security interrupted Claire's thoughts.

Turning around, she met his eyes. "Yes?"

John stood at attention, his hands behind his back in a formal stance. "Perhaps we should hurry if we hope to make it to Parliament on time."

"Thanks. You're right." She shoved her thoughts of inadequacy deep, deep down, and hurried through the walkway to see her final patient for the day. Still, a nagging thought circled her mind. Would she ever be perfect enough? Maybe even queens were unable to hit the mark.

Chapter 7

Claire arrived at the entrance to the Parliament building with two minutes to spare. She had to make a short speech at the end of the meeting, something she'd never gotten used to and still dreaded. Sweat beaded on the back of her neck and trickled down her spine. Thankfully, she'd changed into a black dress, so at least the general public, Maurelle, and the royal family wouldn't see how frantic she felt—she hoped.

John opened the car door for her.

She lifted her eyes to meet his. "Thanks."

"My pleasure, ma'am." He moved aside to let her step out of the car.

Ethan had called her on the way over and told her he'd be late. A family business emergency had arisen, and it had taken him longer than planned to tackle it.

For some reason, a memory of her first day of kindergarten came to mind. She'd taken the school bus because her mother had to go to work, and her father, whom she didn't even know existed at the time, lived across the Atlantic Ocean, preparing to run Amorley himself. As she stepped off the bus and her eyes fell upon the imposing school building, a voice broke through her six-year-old fears, "Honey, you'll do great. I'm cheering you on and praying for you. Besides, if anyone gives you a hard time, they'll answer to me."

Claire had spun around, and there stood Granny wearing a hot pink tracksuit with lipstick to match. The outfit made six-year-old Claire giggle and knowing her granny had driven behind the bus to school sent a wave of relief rushing through Claire.

As if mimicking the memory that had come to mind, Claire's feet remained planted to their spot, allowing her eyes to stare at the foreboding Parliament building.

A welcome voice broke through Claire's inner monologue, "Honey, you'll do great. It will be fine."

Claire grinned and turned around. "Granny, you came. I didn't think you'd planned to attend today."

"If you think I'm letting you take on that royal crew by yourself, you're crazy. Besides, I want to show off my new tracksuit." Granny grinned and gestured to a lime green concoction that would cause the queen mother's lips to purse.

Grateful tears pooled and threatened to spill over. "I love your outfit, and thanks for coming." She glanced at the Parliament building once more. "We'd better head inside and see what awaits us. Ready?"

Granny snickered and looped her arm with Claire's. "Honey, I was born ready."

The pair climbed the stairs to the massive front door.

As Claire crossed the threshold, hundreds of heads turned in her direction. *Oops.* She was late. Again. Claire drew in a deep breath and held it for a few seconds before releasing it. "Here goes nothing." She guided Granny to the front and helped her find a seat in the third row. The first two rows remained reserved for the royal family and the head members of Parliament.

Claire ascended the stairs to the upper level that functioned more as a stage than a forum for ideas. She took her place behind the podium and gripped it for support. Her hands trembled. Clearing her throat, she opened her mouth to speak, and her voice cracked, "Good afternoon. I am honored to be here with you today. Welcome, everyone, to the State of the Country address. I believe Amorley has unified over the past few months, and I am grateful to have been embraced as your queen. The experience of running the country while also working as a surgeon has allowed me to serve in two capacities that I love. While I've learned the Amorley traditions, I'm discovering the right footing, and the future looks—" She pitched to the side.

What just happened?' In the middle of her speech, she must have wiggled her ankle enough that the heel of her shoe broke. Claire gripped the sides of the podium to the point that her knuckles whitened. Maybe no one noticed. Her eyes flicked to the queen mother's face. It paled. A glance at Maurelle's face confirmed Claire's worst fear—she'd fumbled again. "Uh, um, forgive me, where was I?"

A man's voice called from the back of the room, "You were reminding us all of how outdated the Amorley monarchy has become. This instance proves my point. We now have a queen—a figurehead whose role is unclear and who spends half her time running around a hospital instead of striving for her country's interests."

Blood rushed to Claire's face. She squinted. *Who was speaking?* The way the lighting overhead hit her eyes made it difficult to identify the interloper. "What do you mean?" *Stay calm. Don't engage him.*

"Simply put, one of the topics of the State of the Country meeting today should be the role of the monarchy and how Parliament should review its utility. Perhaps, Parliament should consider a democracy with an elected official or at least a new leader. I have it on good authority that your country is nearly bankrupt, thanks in large part to the drain the monarchy has placed on its people." The mysterious speaker stepped forward.

Claire's heart jumped from her chest and landed in her throat. *Lord Chicanery. Why was he doing this? What did he have to gain?* Only days prior, he'd asked her country for money for Maltenstein. What did he know about running a fiscally solvent country? Before she could ask him these questions, he stepped closer.

"Furthermore, and with no disrespect, you've had

several missteps along the way. It's not your fault. You were never really intended to become the queen. Why, even now, you remain unmarried, and the Amorley Constitution clearly states that its ruler must be married within three months of taking the throne, if not already married by the time of their coronation to ensure the promise of an heir."

Claire couldn't restrain her tongue any longer. "What kind of outdated nonsense is that? That I'm only worthy of ruling if I can produce an heir? That I need a man by my side to rule? Besides, I *am* getting married."

The man lifted a shoulder. "For now. What if something happens and you remain single? Then what? Do you dare violate the current Constitution? Of course, one could review the document and decide if it is time to make some changes. If so, one of those amendments might be to investigate the necessity of a monarchy."

Granny jumped up from her seat and waved her rhinestoned handbag overhead. "Treason. Treason, that's what this is right here. I won't stand for it." She turned to the queen mother with fury in her eyes. "Well? Aren't you going to do something? You can't let this yahoo get away with this."

Claire's eyes jumped to where the queen mother sat a few rows in front of Granny.

The queen mother sent Claire a warning glance.

Maurelle rose from her seat. "If I may—"

Claire stood rooted to her spot; her mouth glued

shut.

Every head whipped in the direction of the smooth, confident voice.

Maurelle clasped her hands in front of her waist. "These concerns need to be discussed privately—not publicly at the State of the Country address."

Her shoulders relaxing a smidge, Claire exhaled. Still, it was Maurelle—this couldn't be the end of the discussion.

Maurelle turned to face the head of Parliament. "I suggest the formation of a committee to address any formal concerns about the monarchy, bearing in mind that it provides a long-standing tradition that dates back hundreds of years."

Claire's stomach tensed again. There it was. Sure, Maurelle hadn't offered up Claire's head on a platter, but the insidious suggestion of forming a committee had cracked open the door to Maurelle's potential future.

Still, at least Maurelle had put an end to the spectacle Hans' father had created.

Claire straightened her posture and cleared her throat. "If no one else has anything to add at this time, I'll continue with the address." She paused, and her eyes searched the room for any objections.

After a few seconds of silence, she fixed her eyes on the papers on the podium. "One thing all of us can agree upon is that we want the best for Amorley and its people, and with a country as strong and loyal as

Amorley, I'm confident its future remains bright." Now regarding her own future—she wasn't as confident about that.

Chapter 8

"I don't know what she thought she was doing up there, all hoity-toity. You know that woman has an ulterior motive for breathing." Granny pursed her lips together.

Claire hunched further over the desk in her room, brainstorming ways to salvage the financially sinking ship that was her country and making a list of remaining items to attend to for her upcoming wedding. No big deal, right? Rubbing her forehead, she sent a sidelong glance toward her granny. "Huh?"

Granny crossed her arms in front of her chest and narrowed her eyes. "Now, see? There you go again, ignoring me. I'm trying to save Amorley and your marriage, and you're sitting there studying or something. Pay attention. This is important."

Any time Granny took that stance, Claire paid attention—whether it was when she'd reached into the cookie jar without asking as a little girl or made a significant life misstep as an adult, like now.

Wilson must have picked up on the tension in the

room because he whimpered. He tucked his head under his paws, where he sat in the corner of the room on his dog bed. Smart dog—staying out of it.

"It's not that, Granny. I'm overwhelmed, and I've been sitting here all morning reviewing this financial ledger, but it looks like a foreign language to me. Some of the entries make no sense at all—there's some sort of account called the 'Royal Discretionary Fund' that seems to be the source of most of the expenses. I can't find receipts or any extra notes of entry about the purpose of this money. We can't be spending this much each month running the castle or putting on dinners and formal events. The sum is quite…offensive. No wonder Lord Chicanery said something. If I'd known about this sooner, I'd have investigated it myself."

Granny placed a gentle hand on her granddaughter's shoulder. "You didn't know. All you can do is figure out where to go from here. I still say Maurelle is somehow behind this."

Claire snorted. "You can't prove it, though, and neither can I. I'm focusing on what I can do—attempt to rule as perfectly as possible, strip expenses to the bare bones, and plan the rest of my wedding in my free time."

"Speaking of your wedding, how is that going to factor into this whole winning the public's favor back and not looking like you're a drain on society?" Granny always had a blunt way of putting things.

Claire sent her granny a half-grin. "Thanks for the

reminder." She picked up a magazine sitting next to her and held it so Granny could read the cover.

Granny responded with a tsking sound, "'Weddings on a Budget.' Lovely. That will make for a grand spectacle. Can't wait to see what the newspapers around the world, not to mention the queen mother, have to say about this idea."

Claire shrugged. "What else can I do? I have to show the Amorley people that I'm putting their needs first. This—" she pointed to the magazine cover, "is at least a start."

A knock at the door interrupted the duo's debate.

"Um, forgive me for the interruption, Your Majesty, but you have a visitor downstairs." Albert stood at her bedroom door, his face pale.

Claire raised a brow. "Oh? I wasn't expecting anyone. Who is it?"

Albert wrung his hands together. "Well, uh, Your Majesty, it's Hans Chicanery. He says he's here on urgent Amorley business. I told him you kept a hectic schedule, and he'd have to make an appointment to speak to you in person, but he insisted."

Claire sighed and set her pen down on the stack of papers in front of her. She rose and ran a hand through her blonde locks. "It's fine. I'm not making much headway here anyways. I need a break."

"Ma'am," Albert addressed her but then clamped his mouth shut again.

Closing the space between herself and the head of

the household, Claire locked eyes with him. "Yes? Is there something else?"

Albert's eyes darted to his hands. He held something that he'd rolled into a tube while wringing his hands.

"Is that for me?" Claire asked.

Albert retained a firm grip on the tube. "Before I give this to you, remember that not everyone reads the daily paper, and I'm sure that—"

Claire wrenched it from his hands. As soon as her eyes landed on the front page, she gasped. "No. This is the absolute worst timing. I can't believe they printed this." She pointed at the picture of her standing before Parliament, her lips pursed, and her stance a kilter. The sour look on her face and the shrug of her shoulder gave an overall impression of disinterest. "It is not how it looks. Hans' father ambushed me."

The headline read, "Queen Claire Unconcerned with Amorley's Financial Disaster. Is She the Cause?"

"This is horrible." She whipped around and faced her granny. "What am I going to do?"

Albert cleared his throat. "Ma'am, what should I tell Lord Chicanery's son?"

Claire smacked her forehead. "I almost forgot about him." She grabbed her notebook and papers from her desk, stuffing a few pens inside the binder. Turning around, she blew her granny a kiss. "I'll see you tonight for dinner. I need to deal with Hans and find some way to balance this country's budget, so they don't send me, you, and Wilson back to Boston—or worse, jail."

Granny waved at her granddaughter and clicked her tongue. "Always running around like there's a fire to put out."

The words hung in the air for a few seconds before Claire burst into a fit of giggles. Happy tears sprang to her eyes, and she wiped them away. "Poor choice of words, given that I did cause the dining room to burst into flames not too long ago. The recovery team hasn't even started with the new paint job."

Granny chuckled. "I guess that's true. Sorry about that."

Shaking her head, Claire hurried to her granny and gave her a hug. Lowering her voice close to her ear, she whispered, "I love you."

Her granny gave her a quick peck on the cheek. "Love you, too. Now, hurry. *We* mustn't keep Hans waiting," she said with an upper-crust accent.

Claire smiled and hurried out the door, following Albert down the staircase.

Once at the bottom, Albert turned to her and gestured down the hallway. "He's waiting in the library."

"Thanks." She tossed Albert a grin and headed toward the opulent room, adorned with thousands of books. Ever since Maurelle "accidentally" locked her in the library's secret room, Claire shuddered when she entered it. She loved books and found it a shame that her response to the room felt visceral. Perhaps after the wedding, if they could scrape together enough money to save Amorley's future, she'd redecorate the room. Maybe then Claire could put those terrible thoughts out of her mind. But paint and fabric could only do so much.

Her eyes fell upon Hans' figure seated at the long wooden table in a high-back chair as she entered the room. "Ahem, Albert told me you wanted to speak with me."

Her arrival must have startled him because he shot upright. He turned to face her and gave a slight bow. "Your Majesty. Thank you for seeing me on such short notice."

Claire nodded. "Well, given the events at the State of the Country address, I thought it prudent to have an open, honest discussion. Please," She gestured toward his chair. "Have a seat." Then, she joined him at the table, taking her place at its head.

"Very well, ma'am. As you have been made aware, my father has concerns about Amorley, and as a noble, leader, and businessman, he sees a great opportunity here." The smile on Hans' face looked pasted.

I'm sure he does—like booting me out of my own country before I have a chance to rule. "Go on," she encouraged him.

Hans nodded. "As such, he believes there is much good that he could accomplish for you and the Amorley people. To him, monarchies are a thing of the past—an outdated tradition and a financial drain. I'm afraid, however, I have to disagree with him. I see the value in institutions and historical leadership. Therefore, I'd like to offer you my services as an ambassador or liaison between you and my father." Hans leaned closer, staring intently into Claire's eyes, "I don't think he sees the true value in Amorley's greatest asset."

Claire's mouth went dry. "What would that be?"

Hans' smile widened, and he lowered his voice. "You."

"Oh." Claire shifted in her seat.

A cough came from behind her. "I hope I'm not interrupting anything important," Ethan's voice boomed. He didn't sound upset about intruding on the interchange; he sounded angry.

Claire turned around and looked at her fiancé's face. His sapphire eyes darkened. "Of course, you're not interrupting. Come, join us. Please." She nodded to the chair next to her.

Ethan crossed the room, his footsteps thudding against the floorboards. He pulled out a chair next to Claire. Sending her a questioning look, he crossed his arms in front of his chest and waited for an explanation. "What are you working on in here?"

Claire sent him a smile and nudged some of the financial papers toward Ethan. "Discussing Amorley's future and looking for a solution to its financial woes— or at least a reasonable explanation of how we landed here and what I can do to fix it, so the entire country doesn't come after me with pitchforks and those flames on sticks."

Ethan chuckled, and his furrowed brow softened a bit. "You mean torches?"

Claire's shoulders relaxed. At least he had joked with her—she couldn't have upset him too much. She snapped her fingers. "That's it—pitchforks and torches—which, given the recent propensity for this place to burst into flames, we don't need around here."

Ethan turned and settled his gaze upon Hans across from him. "Good morning. Nice to see you again." He extended a hand, but she noticed the clench of his jaw.

Hans flashed a self-assured grin and shook Ethan's hand. "It is a pleasure. I came to make amends for the spectacle Lord Chicanery made at the State of the Country address and offer my assistance to Claire. Unfortunately, my father carries the blame for Queen Claire having to dig through all these figures today. I told her I felt horrible about how my father handled himself and that I had no intention of assisting in her overthrow."

Ethan narrowed his eyes. "I suppose this is a goodwill gesture then. Nothing more?"

Hans glanced at Claire, letting his eyes linger longer than necessary. "Of course. Nothing more." His eyes flicked to Ethan. "You're a fortunate man."

"Yes, so you've said." Ethan started to say more but paused. Instead, he leaned closer to the table as if inspecting Hans further. "You look familiar. Do we know each other?"

Hans grinned and straightened his posture. "I don't see how. I went to boarding school most of my life in Maltenstein and then attended college at Rudbridge."

Claire peered at her fiancé, and she could tell that he wouldn't drop the matter concerning this spark of recognition with a quick rebuff from Hans. A nagging thought tickled her brain. *Why would Ethan have met Hans before? Was there something Hans wasn't telling her? Could she trust him?* Before she had the opportunity to find answers to these questions, a chair scraped against the floor. Claire looked up, putting away her internal inquisition.

Hans stood and straightened his tie. "I should be going." He turned to Ethan. "Good to see you again." Then, his eyes danced back to Claire's. "Your Majesty." He bowed. "Thank you for allowing me the honor of your audience today. I hope you will require my services in the future and that you'll allow me to help. Good day." Hans bowed again, but as he rose, he sent Claire a subtle wink.

Even though she loved Ethan, heat warmed her cheeks. *Stop it—stop blushing.* She had absolutely no romantic interest in Hans, but the attention flattered her. She was relieved when the door closed behind Hans.

Raising a hand to stop Ethan before he spoke, Claire poured out an explanation, "Before you say anything, I'm sorry. I didn't invite him here. He showed up on my doorstep like an unwanted animal."

Ethan smirked. "You like all animals—I doubt there's any of them that are unwanted by you."

She nodded. "Fair point, but still, I didn't ask Hans for his company. He came to the castle and requested to meet with me, and I thought, given what happened at Parliament, I should sit down with him. Hans told me he only wanted to help me keep the monarchy alive. He said that he and his father have different political opinions, and he disagrees with how his father has handled things."

Ethan tilted his head. "Do you believe him?"

Claire thought for a moment and then nodded.

Making a swirling motion with his finger, Ethan leaned closer. "So, what was going on between the two of you? Is there something I should be worried about?"

Claire shook her head with vehemence. "Absolutely not. I love you, and I cannot wait to spend the rest of my life with you."

Ethan gave a nod. "I trust you; it's him I have reservations about. It's just I can't help but think I know him from somewhere. Have you ever seen someone's face and had a sense of recognition but still can't place them? For some reason, when I look at him, I get a terrible feeling in my gut."

Claire sent him a half-smile. "Are you sure it's not indigestion?"

Ethan stretched his arms over his head and looked up as if searching his mind for the memory. After a few seconds of silence and not retrieving it, he glanced at her again. "No. I know him—I just can't remember how."

Claire shrugged. "Maybe it will come to you, or perhaps he has one of those faces that looks like someone else in the world—like a doppelganger."

"Maybe." Ethan scooted closer to her and lifted a hand to her cheek. He stroked his thumb against it and tilted her chin toward his.

She closed her eyes and breathed in the scent of his musky cologne. A shiver traveled down her spine as he pressed his lips against hers, gently at first and then with more intensity.

He reluctantly pulled away and took her hand in his. Ethan raised it to his lips and pressed them against the back of her hand. His eyes lifted and steadied upon Claire's. "I cannot wait to marry you either." Then, he rose from his seat and gave her hand one more kiss before releasing it. "I must leave but remember what I said—be careful with Hans. I don't trust him or his father."

Claire's cheeks burned again, this time from the passion of their kiss. It stirred the embers of her love for her fiancé. "I'll be careful," she whispered as he walked away. She'd better be careful. Claire suspected she was playing with a greater fire than the dining room inferno when it came to Hans and his family.

Chapter 9

Ethan ran a hand through his hair and leaned back in his chair. He'd been staring at the financial records Claire had given him yesterday after his impromptu run-in with Hans. He still didn't see any clear answers other than the obvious one. Someone in the monarchy had pilfered hundreds of thousands of dollars off the backs of the Amorley people for years. That, and the fact that his wedding date hung in the air with no recent attention to its plans. At this point, it might not happen at all.

A knock at his door provided a welcome distraction.

"Come in," he called.

The doorknob turned, and the door swung open, revealing his best friend and close confidant, Michael Accerly. "I came as soon as I could get away from work. What's the problem? You sounded so secretive on the phone."

Ethan rose and crossed the room to shake Michael's hand. Then, he gestured to the open seat across from his desk. "Please, take a seat, and yes, it's secretive...and important."

Michael grabbed the arms of the chair and sank into it.

Ethan resumed his place in the tufted leather chair behind the desk and shuffled the papers he'd been scrutinizing into a neat stack. Handing them to his best friend since university, he grimaced. "Here, take a look. It's bad."

Accepting the papers, Michael examined them in silence for several minutes. Letting out a low whistle, he stacked them together as Ethan had done and placed them on the desk as if they might burn him. "You're right. It's bad."

Leaning back in the chair again, Ethan rubbed his face with his hand. "I told you. That's why I needed you to come today. I've looked for some explanation that wasn't nefarious, but the only thing I see is a glorified slush fund that Maurelle likely created in the king's name and then used for her personal enjoyment—in excess. Of course, I realize the crown offers some luxuries, but these expenditures are...criminal. It's obvious she's tried to conceal the contents. Still, suppose this information makes it to Parliament's eyes before we have concrete proof of Claire's innocence—or worse—to the newspapers. In that case, it will provide the ammunition Chicanery needs to take down the Amorley monarchy. While I don't understand his motive, I'm sure Maurelle is involved, and I don't trust the man. I'd bet anything his son, Hans, has an objective beyond stealing my fiancée's heart."

Michael shook his head. "Wow. That's a lot to handle. What are you going to do?"

Ethan looked his friend in the eye. "That's where you come in. I need you to find something in the Amorley Constitution that supports the monarchy beyond a refutable doubt. Something that can stop this nonsense about the dissolution of the monarchy and the implementation of a democratic system because I don't think democracy is Hans' father's intent. I bet he wants total control through Maurelle—a presidential dictatorship or an oligarchy. We have to get to the bottom of these financial discrepancies." Ethan pointed to an entry. "Look at this one regarding the annual polo match."

Michael squinted. "So? There was a charity polo match. That doesn't seem odd."

"Right," said Ethan, "but the amount withdrawn for it is too high. I know because Claire helped plan that event. The total cost didn't come anywhere near this figure." Gesturing at the line in the ledger, Ethan continued, "This isn't the only incongruity. I've found several others like this. The sum would be quite large— in the neighborhood of ' hundreds of thousands of dollars. I can't imagine why the items would be so disparate from reality other than for fraudulent reasons."

Michael nodded. "I'll see what I can find. What about your wedding? It's less than two months away. How are the plans coming along?"

Ethan rubbed his jaw. "Not great. Mademoiselle Couture keeps calling for fashion appointments we don't have time to entertain. My fiancée is on the receiving end of another man's attention. Between running to the hospital, Parliament's library, and putting out literal fires at the castle, Claire looks like she's about to fall apart. If this wedding doesn't happen as planned—and successfully in the media's eye—then that will only add to the belief that Claire is an unfit ruler, and the monarchy has reached its end. I can't let that happen."

Michael tapped the papers before him again. "Leave this to me. If there's something to be uncovered, I'll find it."

Ethan smiled. "Thank you, Michael. You always come through. I know you can do it." This wouldn't represent the first time his friend had come to Claire's rescue with his legal knowledge. Michael remained one of the sharpest lawyers in Amorley and had worked in Parliament.

Michael rose from his seat and headed to the door but paused. "Don't lose hope. Thus far, you and I have overcome university exams, coronation mishaps, and a motorcycle escapade. If I had to bet on anyone, I'd bet on you. You're resilient. Plus, God tells us not to fear people. Don't let that pompous windbag, Lord

Chicanery, intimidate you."

Ethan stood and walked to the door to see his friend out. "Thank you. Again. I don't know what I'd do without you."

Michael slapped his friend on the back. "Me neither."

The two friends grinned, and then Ethan became serious. "Be careful. Whoever mismanaged these funds has gone to extraordinary lengths to hide the financial discrepancies. They likely do not want to be found out, and it's hard to anticipate what they might do to keep this information hidden."

Michael's eyes darkened. "Of course. I'll do all the research myself and ensure no one else at the firm or Parliament knows about it. If I find anything, I'll call right away." Then, he exited the room and gave his friend a final wave.

After closing the door behind Michael, Ethan had just returned to his desk when his cellphone rang. Glancing at the name on the screen, he smiled. "Claire? I thought you had meetings today. Are you okay?"

His fiancée didn't answer but instead burst into tears. She blubbered through a few words, but he couldn't understand anything she said.

"Claire, calm down and take a deep breath. It will be all right—whatever it is. What happened? Just tell me, and we will fix it, I promise."

She sniffled. "Th…this can't be fi…fixed."

"Breathe. Take a minute and breathe," Ethan spoke

in a much calmer voice than he felt. Panic started to fill his chest, but he couldn't fall apart—not when Claire remained in such a state.

Claire inhaled and exhaled on the other end of the phone.

"Good. That's better. Okay, now tell me what happened," Ethan begged in the calmest voice he could muster.

She drew in another breath. "I'm at the hospital."

"You're at the hospital. As a doctor or a patient?" Ethan held his breath.

"A...as a pa...patient," she sobbed.

He shot up from his chair, dashed across the room, and grabbed his suit jacket off the rack against the wall. "Is it serious?"

She whimpered. "Ye...yes. Well, not really...I'm not dying or anything."

Ethan shrugged on his jacket and shook his head. Leave it to his physician fiancée to put things in such succinct terms. She measured everything against death. He flung open his door and raced down the hallway, his phone still pressed against his ear. "I'm on my way. Keep talking."

Claire sniffled. "I went on a horseback ride."

He interjected, "I thought you didn't want to ride ever again after the last trek into the Dark Forest with Maurelle." Memories flowed back from only a few months prior when Maurelle had taken Claire out to look for her missing dog, and the ride had ended with

Claire stranded late at night in the Dark Forest—an incident that Claire and Ethan didn't consider an accident on Maurelle's part.

"I hadn't planned on it, but the head of Parliament stopped by and wanted to discuss the current situation. Given the state of affairs, I wanted to provide some diplomacy. Mr. Fulton suggested we take a ride and chat, so we did. Everything went well until we ran into Maurelle on the ride."

Maurelle. Ethan should have known. "What did she do?"

Claire moaned. "She asked me to dismount and look at her ankle because she thought she'd twisted it during her ride. We both got off our horses, and she leaned against my horse while I examined the ankle. Everything looked fine, which I told her, and she informed me that getting out of the stirrups seemed to have helped. Then she thanked me, remounted, and rode away as if all was well."

"I see. How did you end up in the hospital then?" Ethan arrived at his car and opened the door. Ducking his head, he slid inside.

"After Maurelle left, I climbed back on my horse and nudged him to take a few steps forward, but he shot off as soon as my full weight hit the saddle. I tried to hold on for as long as I could, dodging tree limbs and praying he'd stop by some miracle, but—"

"But you fell off." Ethan shoved his keys into the ignition and turned the key. The vehicle roared to life.

"I fell off—that's an understatement. The horse hit a rock or branch or something on the ground with his hoof, and I flew through the air. Thankfully, I landed on my back and arm and not my head, but I probably broke my wrist."

"Maybe you didn't," Ethan encouraged her as he merged into traffic. Streetlights had turned on and twinkled overhead.

"Ethan, I'm an orthopedic surgeon. Unfortunately, I'm pretty sure I did." She sighed and then lowered her voice, "The thing is, I don't think it was an accident."

Ethan's blood went cold. He gripped the steering wheel tighter. "Why? How would your horse running wild not have been an accident?"

Claire whispered, "When Mr. Fulton helped me gather my horse so we could return to the castle for help, the animal acted disturbed—almost as if he was in pain. I looked him over and found a thumbtack pressed into his back on the underside of the saddle near where Maurelle had rested her hand while I examined her foot. She put it there on purpose."

Ethan pressed his foot against the gas pedal, spurring his car to carry him to Claire faster. "I'm on my way. Don't worry—I won't ever let her hurt you again." He hung up the phone and vowed between clenched teeth. *Never again.*

Chapter 10

Ethan burst through the emergency room doors and scanned the hallway, his eyes searching everywhere. His heart had pounded the entire ride to the hospital. How could Maurelle have sunk so low? She could have killed Claire.

A nurse in green scrubs approached him. "Excuse me, but you look lost. May I help you?"

His eyes scoured the area for his fiancée. "Yes, I'm here for Dr. Claire Thomson. She came in a little while ago for a possible wrist fracture."

The older nurse's eyes widened. "Oh," she lowered her voice and leaned forward. "you mean the queen. Only a few of us know that she's here as a patient. We've attempted to keep it hush-hush. Otherwise, the media would descend on this place like a swarm of hornets, and I'm sure she wouldn't want that."

Ethan matched the level of his voice to hers, "I'm sure you're right. Thank you for considering her wishes."

The woman righted herself and gave a flick of her

hand, indicating he should follow. "She's down this hallway in the east wing. I logged her into the system under a pseudonym as well."

Following the nurse, Ethan pondered how quiet he could keep this incident, given that Claire had a recognizable face and worked at the hospital, but at least this nurse had made an effort. *That's all she needs is another picture in the paper.*

The nurse stopped in front of the doorway to the final room and knocked.

A sweet, familiar voice called, "Come in."

The nurse opened the door and revealed her secret patient.

Ethan's stomach plummeted. Claire lay in the bed, her complexion resembling the color of the ecru bedsheet except for a violaceous bruise developing on her left cheek. An imposing knot formed on the left side of her forehead.

Claire's hair, usually shiny, golden, and swept into place, now frizzed out every which way as if she'd done several somersaults before stopping after her fall. "Claire, look at you. This is terrible. Are you sure you didn't hurt more than just your wrist? Perhaps they should do some scans or images or whatever you call them."

She waved a hand at him in protest. "It's not as bad as it looks."

He raised a brow at her. "Have you seen your forehead? You've got a goose egg starting there."

Claire shook her head and winced. "My head should be okay—they did a CAT Scan of it, and I doubt there's permanent damage. My left wrist, unfortunately, did not fare so well. My distal radius is probably fractured. I might have to wear a cast for a while. Wouldn't that look lovely for the wedding?"

Ethan walked over to her and sat on the edge of her bed, taking her good hand in his. He sent her a smile and stroked her hand. "All that matters is that you are alive. I cannot believe that Maurelle did this. You could have died."

Tears pooled in Claire's eyes. "I know, but I didn't. At least now I know what and who I'm dealing with. I won't let my guard down with her ever again."

"No, I suppose not." Ethan tilted his head, examining the casted arm. "At least it's not your good hand. You'll still be able to write, carry things, and maybe even see patients. Although, I guess performing surgery is out of the question."

More tears filled Claire's eyes, spilling over and running down her cheeks in little trails.

Ethan wiped them away with his thumb and leaned forward, pressing his lips carefully against each cheek before landing softly on her lips. The sensation of her mouth against his caused his pulse to quicken. Before they created too much of a scene, he pulled away and whispered, "Don't worry about any of it. We'll figure it out. The first thing I'm going to do is confront Maurelle. She belongs in prison, but I'll settle for banishment again—this time to the ends of the Earth."

Claire squeezed his hand with her good one, her eyes resolute. "You must not say a word to her."

"Why not? We can't have a crazy person living at the castle with us. Who knows what she'll do next?"

Claire turned to face him, wincing at the movement. "I agree with your concern, but if we confront her, she'll deny it, and then she'll know that I'm aware of what she did. I don't want to give her a chance to prepare her defense. It's better that she believes she has the upper hand for now. We still need to find proof of her creative accounting at the castle. Until I have evidence that she did it so I can take it to Parliament, let's allow Maurelle to think she's won."

Ethan frowned. "Very well, but I'd still like to see her put in a cell."

Claire scooted closer to him on the bed. "We don't have the proof, and besides, I don't think there's a jail cell capable of containing Maurelle. She moves like the wind. I don't doubt she could somehow wiggle her way out of it."

A knock sounded at the door, and a doctor entered the room. "Uh, Your Majesty... um, Dr. Thomson—"

Claire interrupted his floundering, "Dr. Jones, we've worked together in this hospital on several occasions. Please call me Claire."

The gentleman's face reddened. "Oh, I don't think I can call the queen of our country by her first name. I'll stick with Dr. Thomson."

Ethan frowned. "What did the x-ray show?"

The doctor handed a copy of the radiograph to Claire so she could see it for herself.

She took it in her good hand, raised it to the light, and groaned. "Not good."

Sending her an empathetic smile, the physician said, "Not good. It's an impressive break, and it requires a cast."

Sighing, Claire returned the x-ray to him. "Fine. After I get the cast placed, can I leave here?"

The doctor nodded. "I'll release you, but you must take it easy and rest for the remainder of the week. The cast has to stay on for at least the next six weeks, possibly eight. No exceptions."

Claire sank back into her pillow. A bit of light left her eyes. "Oh, I'd hoped to remove it before the wedding—it's in six weeks.

"You and I both know that we have to do what's best for your wrist. What would you tell your patients? I'm afraid it's still six to eight weeks. We will have to wait and see how quickly you heal. However, there is good news. Your head CAT Scan came back clear—no bleeds or fractures. Still, you likely have a concussion, so no driving or operating machinery. Be sure to get lots of rest, minimize screens, television, that sort of thing, and avoid mental stress and excessive socialization."

A guffaw erupted from Claire that startled both Ethan and the doctor.

Dr. Jones' brows lifted. "Did I say something amusing?"

Waving her hand in front of her face, Claire calmed herself before answering, "No, it's the part about reducing mental stress and social events—not possible. I have a royal wedding to plan and attend, a country to save, and a monarchy to defend. Oh, and an appointment tomorrow for a total makeover with a petite French woman. If I don't show up for it, my wrist won't matter because she'll have killed me."

The doctor removed his glasses and rubbed his forehead. "I don't want the queen of Amorley assassinated over hair and makeup. However, I doubt you'll feel well enough tomorrow to keep the appointment."

Claire pressed on, "If I relax tonight and feel up to it tomorrow, as long as I promise to sit in a chair the entire time, could I still go?"

Dr. Jones replaced his glasses and shrugged. "Ultimately, the decision is up to you, but don't push yourself too hard or too fast. Take it slow."

Ethan understood how his fiancée felt. They didn't have the luxury of taking things slowly—not if they were going to salvage the crumbling monarchy and thwart whatever evil plans Maurelle and Lord Chicanery had. He rose from the bed. "I'll make sure she rests and doesn't do too much over the next week."

Shifting his weight, Dr. Jones agreed, "That would be good. If you don't have any further questions or need anything else, I must attend to another patient with a fractured leg. Again, please take care of yourself, Your Majesty." He made a slight bow, turned, and exited the room.

Claire shook her head. "I'll never get used to people curtsying and bowing to me. It's weird. Especially from people I work with. He's never bowed before. Because the coronation happened and everything is official, it's caused a shift at the hospital. Well, that's the least of my problems right now."

Ethan stroked Claire's hair and smiled. "Everyone in Amorley adores you, and Dr. Jones wants to be respectful. I'm grateful that your injuries aren't any worse than this. I'll go collect your discharge papers and find a wheelchair to take you to the car." He started to leave, but Claire's hand on his arm stopped him.

"No wheelchair. I'm not an invalid. If I hold onto you, I can walk." Claire sent him a warning look. "I insist."

Twenty minutes later, Ethan pushed Claire in the hospital-mandated wheelchair to the curb of the hospital's emergency room entrance. He locked the chair and walked around to the passenger side door to open it for Claire, then turned and extended a hand to her. "Your chariot awaits."

She frowned at him. "I can't believe you made me ride in the wheelchair."

Ethan shrugged and grinned. "It wasn't my decision. Hospital policy, remember? A hospital at which you work, I might add."

Claire tucked her disheveled hair behind each ear and placed her hand in his. A groan escaped her lips as she rose with Ethan's help and her good hand. Once righted, she collapsed against his chest.

His eyes locked on hers. He tucked a loose strand of hair behind her ear. "I'm glad you are all right. When you called me, I—" His throat tightened, and he took a moment before continuing, "—thought the worst. 'What would I do if anything happened to you? You are the queen of my heart, and I love you."

Claire lifted her lips to his and kissed away his fears and concerns. When she pulled away, a smile tugged at the corners of her mouth. "That is the sweetest and possibly the cheesiest thing I've ever heard."

Ethan chuckled. "What can I say? I'm a hopeless romantic."

Claire's mouth settled into a thin line. "I love you, too, Ethan. So much."

Ethan made way for Claire to take her seat with a flourish of his hand.

She slid inside the car, and once he'd taken his seat as well, they drove away. Tomorrow would bring a new day filled with answers and solutions. *Hopefully*.

Chapter 11

Claire settled into the chair awaiting her in a room that had been turned into a makeshift beauty parlor. Her reflection in the mirror exposed her sentiments about the experience yet to come—dread. She frowned. "I don't know why I have to do this. There's nothing wrong with the way I wear my hair and makeup. This is the way I've always looked."

Mademoiselle Couture patted her arm. "Yes, Your Majesty, and that is the problem—you see nothing wrong. My job is to see the flaws we must correct before your wedding day if, as you have reiterated countless times, you want to be perfect."

Nodding, Claire pulled her shoulders back and submitted to the task. "You're right. I want the day to go perfectly—or at least as close to it as possible. Hopefully, I won't lose my notes or have to jump off a stage or do something else embarrassing in public this time." Her history at royal public events had been sprinkled with various mishaps that always landed her and the Evercliff name on the front page of the newspaper—often not for a positive reason. But this time, she would get it right.

Mademoiselle Couture gave a firm, quick nod. "Exactement." She clapped her hands together. "Let's begin."

Several of Couture's staff hopped into motion, dressed in all-black pantsuits, click-clacking around the room in their high heels. Within seconds two of them flanked Claire's sides, each one carrying an assortment of hair tools and makeup.

Mademoiselle Couture studied Claire's face and hair in the mirror. "Hmm. Well, we must address your hair color."

Claire furrowed her brow. "What's wrong with it? It's blond. Lots of people are blond."

The French woman tilted her head. "It's more flaxen and leaning toward the color of straw—*Pas bon*. We must elevate the color and add some sheen. Also, your complexion—"

Claire couldn't imagine what they could do to change her complexion, but she was more than a little afraid to find out the answer. Sunless tanners didn't fare well for her, and as a fair-complected person, UV rays remained her enemy. She'd go straight from pale to lobster in under a half-hour. "What are you going to do about that?"

Tipping her head to the other side, Mademoiselle barked orders in French to the woman standing on Claire's left. The frightened girl nodded and set her makeup case on the counter, digging through it. She found a tube of liquid and handed it to Mademoiselle Couture.

"Voilà, this is a more appropriate shade for your foundation. What color are you wearing now? It's horrid." Mademoiselle frowned as if Claire's skin had misbehaved on purpose.

Claire shifted in her seat. "Uh, I'm not wearing anything right now. This is my natural skin tone."

"No. Absolutely not." Mademoiselle Couture rebuked Claire's natural state. She and the makeup assistant began spackling their blank canvas with a light beige color.

Twenty minutes passed with Mademoiselle Couture shouting orders in French at the assistants and Claire suffering through multiple layers of brushes splaying colors across her face. After three shades of foundation, two blends of blush, and a near eye jab with a mascara wand, the makeup portion of the debacle concluded.

Mademoiselle Couture clapped her hands again. "Now your hair. It needs lightening, for certain." She lifted a limp lock and narrowed her eyes. "I dare say—"

She didn't dare say anything because before she could pontificate on the miserable attributes of Claire's coif, a menacing voice called from behind, "My, my, it looks like you've recovered well."

The blood in Claire's veins turned to ice. She shivered, and her eyes drifted upward toward the reflection of her stepmother in the mirror. "Yes, Maurelle, I have. Thank you." Lifting her casted hand, Claire gave it a wave. "Nothing a few hours in the hospital and several pain killers couldn't manage."

Nodding, Maurelle sent Claire a forced smile. "Wonderful. Glad to hear it. What do you have underway now?"

Mademoiselle Couture clucked her tongue. "We are in the middle of a transformation for her wedding day, and you are interrupting our work." The French woman never shied away from a battle, regardless of her foe. Even though Maurelle terrified most people, Couture viewed her as merely an impediment.

Maurelle put a hand to her chest and widened her eyes. "Oh, please don't mind me. I didn't mean to interrupt. I only came here to inform you that the wedding dress has returned from the seamstress and is waiting with Albert in the front hall. I thought you might want to attend to it, Mademoiselle Couture, before Wilson has a chance to leave his mark on it."

Mademoiselle Couture's brow raised to her scalp. "That wretched animal cannot destroy this dress! I won't stand for it." She clapped her hands again, and the two assistants righted themselves as if standing at attention in the army. "Come with me, ladies. We must secure that dress before it falls to ruin." Then, she turned to Claire and narrowed her gaze. "Don't move. I'll be right back. We are not finished."

Claire didn't budge, but her eyes flicked toward

Maurelle in the mirror once again, and she caught her gaze. "Thank you for letting us know about the wedding gown." Perhaps Maurelle would take the hint and leave.

Her stepmother sidled closer to the temporary makeup counter, her' fingers grazing across several of the pieces of makeup and tools. "Well, they've gone to a lot of trouble to turn you into a proper queen for your wedding day. Do you think everything will be 'perfect'?" Maurelle's inflections were always subject to interpretation.

Claire knew better. "I hope so."

A loud crash sounded from the hallway, and a mixture of French and English yelling followed. *"Oh la la la la, Albert!"* Mademoiselle Couture did not sound pleased at all.

Jumping from her chair, Claire ran to the hallway to rescue Albert from Mademoiselle's clutches. Bursting through the entryway, Claire's eyes landed on the source of the ruckus.

Wilson had somehow wrestled the dress bag from Albert's hands and now had it gripped firmly between his teeth. His fluffy tail wagged at the comedy he'd created.

Claire could tell within seconds that he planned to run off, ready to create a game of chase. "Wilson, stay," she warned.

The dog lowered his head to the ground and wagged his tail faster.

"Drop it," she urged, this time with more force.

Wilson stared at her as if determining whether or not Claire was serious. After a few seconds, his tail stilled, he stood and dropped the garment bag before trotting down the hall, likely in search of some other inappropriate item to devour.

Claire sighed. She walked over and retrieved the dress bag, handing it to Albert. "No harm done."

Mademoiselle Couture huffed, "That remains to be seen. Honestly, that animal does not belong inside the castle. I've said it time and time again, but no, we must bow to the canine's wishes. I can't believe I've reduced myself to chasing after a dog." She started toward the makeover room, still muttering, "I could have shown a collection in Paris, but no, I accepted the invitation to adorn this circus. My mother was right. I should have married that count when I had the chance." She stomped the rest of the way down the hall.

Claire followed behind, clamping a hand over her mouth. A chuckle erupted and threatened to turn into a full-out guffaw, but thankfully Granny wasn't around to urge it on. After composing herself, Claire entered the room and took her seat in front of the mirror once again.

Maurelle had vanished—no small blessing.

Mademoiselle Couture drew in a deep breath and released it. "Where were we?" She glanced at the top of Claire's head. "Oh, that's right. This horrid hair. Let's fix it.'"

Claire raised a brow. "It won't look too different, will it? I still want to feel like myself."

Mademoiselle Couture placed a hand on Claire's shoulder. "Trust me, anything I do will only improve upon the situation." Then, she got to work, picking up a bowl that held a greyish purple paste. She stirred it with a brush and painted the concoction on Claire's hair. Once she'd covered all of Claire's hair with several silver foils, Mademoiselle Couture placed a towel on top of Claire's head and shifted her away from the mirror. "It's best not to look until the end. It will be a surprise."

Claire nodded and stayed put while Mademoiselle Couture cleaned up the area. The two assistants bustled about the room, packing things in suitcases and carrying some of the items out of the room.

Forty-five minutes later, Mademoiselle Couture spun Claire around and announced, "Voilà." She removed the towel from Claire's head and gasped.

Claire stared at her sapphire-blue reflection, and her mouth dropped open. "Wha...what happened? Is it supposed to look like this?"

Mademoiselle Couture pulled the foils out of Claire's hair, revealing that her entire head was indeed blue. "Get over here and wash this out at once," she shouted at her assistants.

Two women dashed over and guided Claire to the sink. They pushed her down and got to work, attempting to wash away the cerulean color.

Thirty minutes and a lot of French-laden yelling later, Claire's hair remained blue. She raised her brow, tears filling her eyes. She had never been a vain woman, but she couldn't relish the idea of walking down the aisle, seeing patients, or addressing Parliament with blue hair. It was the exact opposite of perfection. "What am I going to do? I can't go out in public like this.'"

Granny entered the room as Mademoiselle Couture and her assistants launched into a complicated discussion about repairing the damage. "He-hah. I don't see why not. It's wonderful—absolutely fantastic. You now have something new and blue in one shot."

"Granny, I know you think you're funny and improving the situation with humor, but this is not how I want to keep to wedding traditions—with hair dye."

Mademoiselle Couture's head shot up. "Well, we can't leave it like this for long, but I cannot apply another round of bleach to the hair tonight. We might fry it all off your head."

Claire's hand flew to her damp blue hair. "I don't want to be bald. So, now what?"

Mademoiselle Couture glanced at the assistant holding the hairdryer and nodded. "We dry it and cover it with a fashionable scarf or hat for now, and you go straight to bed. That way, the paparazzi won't get a whiff of this. You can take dinner in your room. Then, tomorrow first thing, I'll straighten it out myself."

"How did this happen?" Claire fingered a blue

tendril, her mouth still agape.

Mademoiselle Couture's face clouded. "I don't know. Victoria has been working with me for years, and this has never happened before. If I didn't know better, I'd say that someone tampered with the hair dye, but that's simply impossible."

A nagging thought tickled Claire's mind. *Maybe not so impossible.* Maurelle had stayed in the makeover room when they'd all rushed away to the chaos in the hallway with Wilson. "Hmm." Claire frowned.

Mademoiselle Couture and her assistants left her after they'd finished making her hair look as respectable as possible—which was to say, blown out straight but still sapphire.

Once the trio had left the room, Claire lowered her voice to a whisper, "Granny, I think I know how my hair ended up like this."

Granny dipped her head and joined in a reciprocal, conspiratorial voice, "Oh? How?"

Claire glanced around to ensure they remained alone. Once assured of no eavesdroppers, she launched into an explanation of the previous twenty-four hours' events. She started with the wild ride and fall due to the misplaced thumbtack and ended with her unexplainable hair-dye job. "I know it sounds like a leap to assume she tampered with the saddle and the hair dye, but at this point, I wouldn't put much past Maurelle."

Granny snorted. "Honey, neither would I. So, what are we going to do about it? Want me to dump some green food coloring in her shampoo?" A wicked twinkle filled Granny's eye.

Claire grinned but didn't want to encourage her granny. "I'm not sinking to her level."

"So what? Should we do nothing then? Let her get away with it? She's going to bad-mouth you to the country and Parliament until you're totally out of a job." Granny tsked.

"I never said we should let her get away with it, but she'll deny any involvement if we confront her now. Plus, it will put her on guard. I want her to think she's gotten away with everything while I'm investigating the financial nonsense." Claire stared out the window, considering her problems. "No, tomorrow Mademoiselle Couture will fix my hair, and hopefully, no one else will find out about this disaster. There's nothing I can do to hurry along my wrist's recovery. I may have to wear a cast to my wedding. Won't that look grand?"

Her granny draped a thin arm around Claire's shoulders and gently squeezed her granddaughter. "You'd look grand in a brown paper bag. Don't worry about the cast. Now, what's this I hear about Wilson stealing another dress?"

Claire shook her head and smiled. "Thankfully, that turned out all right—I think. Wilson grabbed the wedding dress bag, but he didn't do any damage. I thought Albert might have a stroke, though. You should have seen the look on his face."

Granny chuckled. "Good ole Albie. Poor guy. Your dog keeps him busy."

"Yes, at least he's a good sport about it all." Claire chuckled.

"Right." Granny stared at Claire's hair again before adding, "Are you sure you don't want to hit up a rock concert tonight? It seems like a waste of a daring hairdo to go straight to bed."

Claire laughed and stood from her chair. She took Granny's hand in hers and turned, heading for the staircase and the safety of her bedroom. "No. I think not. Can you imagine the newspapers tomorrow with that picture? You and me at a concert, me with blue hair and a cast, and you in your monochromatic red tracksuit?"

Granny shook a finger at Claire. "Listen, you might be the queen, but I won't tolerate you making fun of my tracksuits. They are comfortable and make a bold fashion statement."

Claire laughed again. "That they do, Granny."

After Granny headed to bed, Claire whispered a quiet prayer that the week wouldn't bring any more surprises.

Chapter 12

Ethan pulled up to Evercliff Castle, briefcase in hand. Inside, it held the latest results from Michael's research into the financial inconsistencies of the monarchy. He waited at the front door, his heart racing.

Albert opened the door. His eyes widened, and his face pale. "Lord Ethan Kane. I didn't know we were expecting you today."

Nodding, Ethan stepped inside. "I hadn't planned to come over today because Claire told me she had a hair crisis this week or some other Mademoiselle Couture obligation. I didn't want to get involved lest she decides to make me over as well." He chuckled.

Albert didn't seem to get the joke. "Right. Of course. Uh, have you spoken to Queen Claire since her accident?"

Ethan frowned and straightened his tie. "No, I dropped her off from the hospital and told her I had business to attend to in the city. I wanted to discuss recent developments regarding something confidential with my colleague." His brow furrowed further. "Why?

Is she all right?"

Albert paused before answering and placed his fingertips together. "Well–"

Shooting straight upward, Ethan took a step closer to Albert. "What happened? She can't have had another injury."

Shaking his head, Albert continued, "Her Majesty is not hurt, although I should say the cast on her arm is enough for one week."

Ethan gave a cautious smile. "Right. So, then what is it?"

Instead of responding, Albert gave a flick of his hand. "Perhaps you'd better come with me and see for yourself. There was a small...mishap."

Ethan fell in line behind Albert, his heart pounding harder in his chest. What could have happened overnight? This would be Maurelle's final move if he had anything to do about it. He'd go to Parliament today and make a formal accusation. "I wish you'd tell me what is going on. I—" Ethan froze, and his mouth fell open at the sight before him.

Claire sat in a wingback chair in the library, staring at a pile of papers in her lap.

Albert cleared his throat. "Your Majesty, Lord Ethan Kane has arrived and requests a moment of your—"

Ethan dropped his briefcase, interrupting Albert's formal introduction, "Your hair is blue. No, it's not just blue. It's sapphire. What—what—was this intentional?"

She peered up at him. "Of course, it wasn't intentional. Add it to the list of things I suspect of Maurelle orchestrating, but yet again, I have little proof in hand." Claire stacked the papers into a neat pile and leaned back in the chair, crossing her arms in front of her chest.

Even though this woman before him bore a closer resemblance to the tapestries than his betrothed, he found her dazzling. Her blue eyes flashed, and a flush filled her cheeks that flattered her. "I missed you, and I'm thankful that you are all right. Forgive me for being so consumed with work this week. When Albert told me there'd been another incident, I couldn't imagine—"

"That your fiancée had dyed her hair and looked more fit for a rock concert than a chapel?" She sent him a small smile and then placed her paperwork on the table next to her chair. "Mademoiselle Couture has tried to fix it all week, although unsuccessfully." Standing, she crossed the room and fell into his arms, taking care with her casted arm. As it bumped against his chest, she winced.

"Does it hurt?" He stared into her eyes.

"Not too bad—only a little. Don't worry about the hair. Mademoiselle Couture is supposed to return later today. She promises to have found a secret solution that will do the trick. At this point, I'd settle for any shade resembling natural hair color."

Ethan lifted a strand of Claire's locks and let it fall between his fingers. "Oh, I don't know. I could get used to it." He chuckled.

Claire swatted his shoulder with her good hand. "Very funny. No, when the queen mother saw it, I thought she'd faint. Of course, Granny found it hilarious and thinks it makes the perfect statement for the wedding. I believe her exact words were, 'It shows a great display of patriotism.' So, there's that."

Tipping his head toward her, Ethan gave Claire a soft, quick kiss. "I agree with Granny." He lost himself in her eyes for a minute before recalling the cause of his trip. "Well, now that we have your hair fiasco settled, I have something to show you." He released his soon-to-be bride and bent down to retrieve his briefcase. Then, he walked over to the two chairs where Claire had been sitting when he'd entered the room.

She took her place opposite him and waited.

He opened the briefcase and pulled out a large file, pausing before handing it to Claire. "Michael delivered this to me this morning. He said he'd discovered something quite shocking. I took a look at the papers, too, and he's right."

Claire took the file from him, opened it, and flipped through the pages one at a time. Her eyes skimmed each page, her face transforming from perplexed to infuriated. After several minutes, she raised her head. "No. It can't be true. All this time?"

Nodding, Ethan confirmed her assessment. "All this time. Maurelle has been using a shell company to create a slush fund for herself since she married your father. Michael might not have ever figured it out, but he found one cleared check with the initials MEE in the signature line. It appears that she created a company under the pretense of a charitable organization and titled it the Amorley Care Fund under the umbrella of the Royal Discretionary Fund. He couldn't find any information about the organization other than the mission statement, which explained the company existed to assist the Crown and its fellow citizens. Each deposit into the fund appears to have come from an operational fee under the general tax. The withdrawals from the fund occurred at regular intervals each month. The small sum remained the same each time except for the check bearing the MEE signature."

Claire raised her head and arched a brow. "What was different about that one?"

Ethan pointed to a few papers further down in the stack, revealing a copy of the check. "That one was for a much larger amount and happened right after your father passed away. I suspect Maurelle had been using the fund for her expenditures, and with your father's passing and you possibly becoming the future heir to the Crown, she took an advance of sorts in case things didn't go her way."

"Can you prove that MEE is Maurelle?" Claire asked.

Ethan frowned. "I can't. However, Michael found a small footnote in one of the columns referencing a letter from MEE to Lord Chicanery. Do you think

Maurelle could have been communicating with him for a long time? Perhaps, he knows something about this or has a hand in it?"

"But why do you think that it's Maurelle's initials?" Claire glanced at the papers once more.

"Because I noticed something. All of the entries in the ledger contain the same handwriting except for the ones with the larger sums. Those had initials that looked familiar to me, so I went home and dug through my family's desk in the study. I thought I'd seen the handwriting before."

Claire lifted her forehead. "And?"

"I found a thank you note Maurelle sent to my father after he donated money at a charity ball the Crown held. It contained the signature of your father and hers. The M's matched. I'm convinced that it's her handwriting." Ethan sat back in his seat, finished stating his case.

Claire shook her head. "Wow. I wish I could say that I can't believe it, but I'd believe anything she did after the past year. However, we need more proof than a similar M."

Ethan clasped his hands together and leaned forward. "You're probably right. I'll tell Michael to keep looking and see if he can turn up any further traces of communication. Maybe you can look around the castle and see if she's left any evidence here. In the meantime, keep that paperwork in a safe place away from her eyes. If she finds out that we're on to her, she'll do whatever it takes to defend herself."

"Right." Claire rose from her seat and climbed several rungs up a ladder in the library that leaned against a shelf of books. She pulled out several thick reference books from the top shelf. Standing on her tiptoes, Claire tucked the paperwork into the back of the ledge and replaced the encyclopedias. She took a few careful steps down but caught her heel on a lower rung.

Ethan rushed to her side and caught her in his arms. "Careful. You've had enough injuries for a lifetime. Let's make it down the aisle with you in one piece." He searched her lovely face, caressing it with his eyes. "I cannot wait to marry you."

"I can't wait to marry you either. And thank you for saving me. Again."

He gently sat her down on the floor and leaned closer, pressing his lips against hers. His pulse quickened.

Claire melted into his arms.

She renewed his hope that a bright future was still possible. As they parted, he squeezed her hand. He whispered close to her ear, "I love you. Be careful."

She kissed him on the cheek. "I love you, too, and I will."

Ethan reluctantly stepped away and hurried out of the castle to his car, ready to search for more proof of Maurelle's underhanded ways. Then he'd find a way to salvage the monarchy's financial security and reputation. He wouldn't rest until he'd vanquished

Claire's stepmother once and for all.

Chapter 13

Claire watched as Ethan exited the room. Sighing, she heaved herself from the chair she'd sat in for the past several hours, poring over unintelligible financial paperwork. She checked around the room to ensure she hadn't forgotten any forms on the table. Her eyes landed on a book that stuck out from the others on the top shelf near where she'd hidden her papers.

Crossing the room, Claire stared upward at the text. It looked old, tattered, and protruded two to three inches further than the other books. She couldn't reach it from the ground, so she pulled around the ladder. A few seconds later, she perched herself at the top of the ladder and retrieved the tome. It felt bulky, and though she tightened her grip on it as she stepped down, the book slipped from her grasp. It fell, and when it struck the floor, it opened, and several worn papers folded in half flew out of it.

How odd. Claire continued down the ladder and picked up the book once she'd reached the bottom. Turning it on its side, she noted that it was an outdated reference book on the monarchy's hereditary succession. She set the text on the ground to gather up the stray forms.

Unfolding the papers, Claire skimmed the words on them. She gasped. A wave of nausea swept over her. She read them a second time, unable to believe what she'd seen.

"My, my, you certainly don't stop for anything, do you? After you fell off the horse and then suffered the unfortunate incident with Mademoiselle Couture, I suspected you'd stay in bed all week to recover," Maurelle's voice dripped with disdain.

Claire shoved the papers behind her back as she spun around and took a step forward to block Maurelle's prying eyes from the book on the floor. "It's nice of you to share your concern for me, but I'm fine. With the wedding only weeks away and Parliament's concern about the monarchy's finances and the relevancy of its existence, I didn't think it wise to take too many days to rest. Don't you agree?" Sweat dripped down Claire's back and caused her gauzy blouse to stick to her skin.

"Yes, of course. That's right—not much time left at all. Are you ready?" Maurelle raised a brow and gave a nod toward Claire's still-blue hair.

Oh, right. That. Claire would have to see Mademoiselle Couture later today to rectify the hair situation before tackling her more significant problems. "Absolutely. I am confident that the wedding will be a success, and Parliament will see that I have done nothing wrong."

Maurelle stared at her stepdaughter for a moment before turning her attention to her red fingernails. "Hmm. Well, let's hope so." Then, she spun around and sashayed out of the library and down the hallway.

Once her stepmother had left, Claire collapsed to the floor in a puddle. *That was close—too close.* Shaking her head, Claire couldn't believe what she'd seen on these hidden papers. She had to find Granny and call Ethan to share her findings with them. However, first, she must rectify her coif and gather her thoughts. She nodded. Yes, she had a plan.

Rising from her position, Claire folded the papers and shoved them in her pocket, then replaced the large book on the shelf.

Claire ran up the stairs and to her bedroom, closing the bedroom door behind her. Scanning the room for the perfect hiding place where Maurelle wouldn't discover the papers, and neither would Wilson, as he'd love nothing more than to chew them to bits. Claire settled on shoving them between the box spring and mattress on her bed. A quick call to Ethan and she convinced him to agree to meet her first thing in the morning after breakfast. Next up on her agenda to create the perfect wedding—fixing her hair.

~

Claire ate the last bite of a biscuit and took a final sip of Earl Gray tea before wiping her mouth with her napkin. She and Ethan hadn't seen one another for over a week, thanks to unforeseen plans made by Mademoiselle Couture and a mini-crisis at Ethan's work. After several reschedules, today, she'd finally show him what she'd discovered in the library.

Albert appeared at her side to retrieve her dishes.

"Thank you. Please tell the cook the biscuits tasted delicious as always." Claire sent him a smile.

Albert bowed and returned her grin. "Certainly, Your Majesty. Lord Ethan Kane is at the front door. I did not know that he had planned to join you for breakfast this morning. Should I bring him out a place setting and a platter of biscuits?"

Claire shook her head. "He's not here for breakfast. We had something to discuss and had planned to take a short walk in the royal gardens."

Albert bowed again. "Very well, ma'am." Then, he turned to leave.

No matter how many times Claire had asked Albert to call her by her first name, he usually refused. She doubted she'd ever get used to all the 'Your Majesty' stuff.

A few minutes later, Ethan appeared in the doorway, and she had to restrain herself from running into his arms. Attempting propriety and queen-like behavior, Claire rose from her seat and crossed the room calmly before flinging her arms around her fiancé's neck. She inhaled his scent of sandalwood and spices and exhaled, releasing some of her fears. "I've missed you."

Ethan pressed his lips against her cheek. "I've missed you, too." He glanced around the room, still locked in an embrace with Claire. "Where's Granny?"

"Here I am, you two lovebirds, though I don't see why you'd want an old bird like me raining on your romantic parade through the gardens. Wouldn't you rather be alone to smooch?"

Claire spun toward Margaret Thomson. "Granny!"

Granny's eyes sparkled with mischief. "Can't do it. It's not in me." She chuckled before adding, "Well, let's get this show on the pebbled path."

"I don't think that's how the saying goes," Claire chided.

"It's how my saying goes. Let's scoot. You've little time left until your wedding, and if Maurelle and old Hans Sr. have anything to say about it, not only will you not be walking down the aisle, but you'll be on the next flight out of here as you turn in your key to the castle and your crown. We can't have that—so, let's hurry."

The trio dashed down the hallway and out the rear castle door. The midsummer blooms of the garden welcomed them.

Claire pulled in a deep breath, and the fragrance of honeysuckle tickled her nose. Its sweetness buoyed her spirits and made the coming blows of what she had to share with Ethan and her granny a little softer.

"Well, let's have it. What's the big news?" Granny raised a brow and took hold of Ethan's arm to steady her footing on the stony path.

Claire glanced behind her to ensure that no one had followed them. Then, she launched into her escapades in the library after Ethan had left the previous day. As she concluded with the bit about Maurelle nearly catching her as she'd uncovered the old papers, Ethan and Granny stopped walking.

Ethan spoke first, "What did the papers show?"

Claire pulled the folded documents out of her skirt pocket and opened them. She handed them to Ethan. "It's a financial record that's a bit more, uh, frank than the one Michael unearthed."

Ethan's eyes skimmed the pages, and he let out a low whistle. "I'll say. This is a play-by-play of all the mishandlings, purchases, and deductions Maurelle has made since she married your father. I can't believe she left it unguarded in the library."

Claire shrugged. "I guess she doubted anyone would look through the old reference books on the top shelf. I almost had to climb Mount Everest to get to it. Judging by how yellowed the paper is, I'd say it's been untouched for some time. Perhaps, she's even forgotten about its existence."

Granny screwed up her face. "I don't understand why Maurelle would document her no-good tricks. Why put the sins, so to speak, in black and white? Why not just steal the money and leave no trail of it? This way, if someone finds this form as you did, then she's caught."

Claire frowned and shifted her weight. "That puzzled me at first, too. However, I think she probably wrote down her actual expenditures and withdrawals and then made the record Michael found. She probably copied the exact sums with different entries and initials so that the money balanced with the budget in the end."

"What is it those federal agents say? She cooked the books." Granny looked at Claire and grinned.

Claire fiddled with the edge of her blouse. "Something like that. I don't know why she didn't burn up this copy years later, but as I said, maybe Maurelle hid the papers in the book and forgot about them. Based on her past track record, she's pretty bold. I doubt it ever occurred to her she'd ever get caught."

Granny snorted. "Well, won't she be surprised?"

Claire placed a hand on her granny's arm. "We can't say anything to her yet."

Granny's head pulled back, and her eyes clouded. "Why not? That woman has it coming to her, and I can't wait to see her fall. She's almost killed you at least twice—and dyed your hair blue. Maurelle has publicly humiliated you and attempted to steal your birthright. That lady deserves to go down." Granny gave a firm nod of her head.

Claire opened her mouth to speak but then paused.

"Oh, no. There's more, isn't there?" Ethan asked.

"Well, I found another letter—a lengthy one. I

couldn't fit everything in my pocket, so I left it in my room, but it indicated a desire from Hans' father to join forces with Maurelle to take over the Crown. Well, that's not exactly true—he asked her to marry him once she'd forced me out of the way and became queen. Then, there's a second letter indicating that since Maurelle had been unsuccessful in that effort, he would come here to help her remove the monarchy and conquer Amorley. He wanted to set up a democracy and have Maurelle elected as president or some other top-official name, and then he'd planned to marry her and unite his country with ours. He craves power and control—and whatever remains of Amorley's monetary funds. Plus, there are the crown jewels. His country has plenty of land, but it is struggling financially."

Granny snorted. "So, it's what you call a win-win for him. He gets whatever money Maurelle hasn't pilfered yet and power in one shot."

"Exactly. I guess being fifth in line for his country's leadership left him impatient. Perhaps, he thought if he served Amorley on a platter to Maltenstein's ruler, then he'd increase his rank there as well." Claire let her suspicions sink in for Ethan and Granny.

Ethan returned the papers to Claire and waited while she shoved them in her pocket once more. "So, now what?" he asked.

Claire lifted her chin. "Now, we fight."

Granny guffawed. "Ooh, now that's what I like to

hear." She stretched out a hand, waiting for Claire and Ethan to take her lead.

Claire stared at her fiancé, and a slow grin tugged at the corners of her lips. Then, she placed her hand on top of Granny's.

Ethan joined the Thomson girls and stacked his hand on the pile before affirming, "We fight. Maurelle, Hans, and his father won't win no matter what. Soon, Claire and I *will* marry, and we *will* clear the monarchy's name."

Chapter 14

Weeks passed without event, considering that Claire, Ethan, and Granny had uncovered a pending coup. Between using the time to solidify her case, plan her wedding, and run the country, the days blurred into a whirlwind of hectic activity.

Now mere days before her wedding, Claire's hands trembled as she readied herself for the Evercliff Royal Engagement Dinner. She sat in front of her dressing table, putting her earrings in before heading downstairs. According to the queen mother, the dinner was a tradition for the betrothed couple's families to gather and show support for the upcoming union.

"Knock-knock. Can I come in?" Granny's voice echoed from the other side of Claire's bedroom door.

"I'm ready. Come in," Claire replied. She took one final peek at her reflection and smiled. Her blonde locks had been restored, thanks to Mademoiselle Couture after several rounds of her secret solution and some goo that smelled awful but did the job.

Granny's eyes caught Claire's in the mirror, and

tears glistened from her cheeks. "Oh, my dear, you look wonderful. Gorgeous. Although, I didn't mind the blue—found it daring myself."

Claire turned in her seat to face her granny. "Thanks for the unconditional encouragement, but I don't want my televised royal wedding remembered as the one where the bride literally wore blue."

Granny glanced at the gaudy gold watch on her left wrist. "We'd better go, or your other grandmother will be in a huff."

Claire rose and nodded. "Remember, Granny, don't say a word to Maurelle about the financial papers—not one word. I go before Parliament tomorrow and present my case for the monarchy, and I don't want to tip her off beforehand."

Granny scowled. "I can't believe you'd suggest that I'd blab. I'm a vault."

Claire snorted, took her granny's arm, and headed out the bedroom door.

Granny swatted Claire's hand. "Oh, hush. These lips will keep your secret. On a happier note, are you excited about your wedding? I can't believe it's in three days."

"Me either. I can't wait until the Maurelle and Lord Chicanery mess is behind me. I want to enjoy my wedding with a little less scrutiny and scandal. At least I hope we can put the scandal behind us before the ceremony." Claire frowned.

The pair walked down the hallway and carefully

descended the staircase. The sound of tinkling glasses and chattering voices came from the Great Hall, which substituted as the Grand Banquet Room until the completion of the formal dining area's repairs from the fire.

Albert joined their side as Claire and Granny approached the Great Hall. "If I may, Your Majesty, I'll escort your granny to her seat and then return to announce you."

She nodded. The pomp and circumstance still proved foreign to Claire, but she went along with it when possible.

Albert took Granny to her seat across from the queen mother and Ethan. Then, he returned and bowed to Claire before facing the long table filled with over fifty of their guests. "May I present Her Majesty, Queen Claire Thomson."

The entire room rose to its feet in unison. The sound of chairs scraping against the floor echoed throughout the room.

Claire walked to her seat, smiling and giving a slight nod to the familiar faces she passed on her way. Once she'd arrived at her destination, she addressed the room, "Thank you for joining us to celebrate our upcoming wedding. It brings Ethan and me great joy to share this special time with our families. Please, have a seat and enjoy."

The entire room followed Claire's lead and took their seats, and the light chatter resumed. Within seconds a flurry of waitstaff surrounded the table, filling water goblets and offering the first round of appetizers.

Ethan's father sat a few chairs down from Claire. "Well said. It's a shame you had to move the dinner due to the fire. How are the renovations coming along?" He sent her a small smile.

His grin proved nothing short of a small victory for Claire, given their history. For a long time, he'd fought against the idea of a union between his son and the future Queen of Amorley. This idea had perplexed her as well as many in the castle. Eventually, Claire had learned that Ethan's father had been rivals with her father when they were younger, and a major source of contention had been Alexander Evercliff winning over the affections of Claire's mother, Mona Thomson. Thankfully, though, they'd all come to an understanding, and at least Ethan's family contentions had subsided. She doubted Richard, Ethan's brother, and Ethan would ever become best friends, but at least tensions had thawed considerably.

Claire waited while one of the servers placed a strange-looking puff pastry—a whipped salmon concoction—on her plate. Once the waiter had moved on, she turned her attention to Ethan's father, still side-eyeing the appetizer. "Yes, the repairs are well underway. I wish we could have held this dinner in the formal dining room. Here's hoping the workers finish the work in the next few days so we can have a post-wedding breakfast there, but we will see how much headway the contractor makes in the next day."

Hans' father sat opposite Ethan's father and looked like the picture of aristocracy with his black dinner jacket and bowtie. He also wore a sash indicating his title from his home country of Maltenstein. "Yes, it is a shame about the room, especially since it was such an unfortunate accident when Queen Claire bumped over that candlestick. What are the chances of such a thing happening?"

Maurelle sat nearby and would never miss an opportunity to comment on Claire's failures. "I'd say they're about as likely as one's hair turning blue—wouldn't you agree, Your Majesty?" She regarded Claire from under lowered lashes, and a small smirk formed on her lips.

Claire's pulse quickened. She popped the disgusting salmon puff in her mouth to stall for time so she wouldn't say the first thing she'd thought—something unladylike, unqueenlike, and unqueen-mother approved.

After she'd swallowed the repulsive item, Claire smiled at her stepmother. "I'd say you're right. Blue hair—wouldn't that be a sight? Of course, I'd imagine that's a challenging color to achieve without the help of a professional stylist or a special assistant. Wouldn't you agree?" It was the first time Claire had hinted that she'd known or at least suspected Maurelle had a hand in the hair debacle.

Maurelle dabbed her mouth with her napkin and returned it to her lap. "Yes, I'd imagine so. One never can be too careful with such things."

Claire sent her an even stare. "No, one can't."

Granny must have sensed the tension building in the room, and though she loved a good fight, she likely wanted to help Claire survive the evening without making the morning paper—at least not in a negative way. "Well, let's raise our glasses to good hairstylists—to Mademoiselle Couture and the people who will make this beautiful young lady shine on her wedding day—to Claire, Queen of Amorley. Long live the queen." Then, she lifted her crystal water goblet in the air and waited for everyone else at the table to join her.

The group raised their glasses and chanted together, "Long live the queen."

Claire ducked her head, feeling her cheeks warm. She met her granny's gaze and mouthed a silent, "Thank you."

Granny didn't reply other than to send her granddaughter a quick, subtle wink.

Claire grinned.

Ethan reached over and grabbed Claire's hand, squeezing it. "I'm glad you're happy. It's been a challenging few weeks, but everything will work out well."

Claire's palms dampened. "I hope it goes perfectly. I want to prove myself to Parliament—to show them the monarchy remains unblemished and capable of carrying Amorley into the future—and that I'm deserving as their queen. Not to mention I don't want to let down my fellow citizens and colleagues at the hospital. A lot is riding on the meeting with Parliament and the wedding—they both have to be perfect."

Ethan looked into Claire's eyes. "They will—even if they don't go as planned. You don't have to be perfect. You only have to be yourself. That's enough—more than enough. I love you."

Claire leaned closer and whispered, "I love you, too."

The rest of dinner went surprisingly well. Claire managed to navigate the evening without catching anything on fire or her dog eating the main entrée, so she considered the event a win. With a sigh, she ate the final bite of a piece of delicious chocolate cake, her favorite dessert. Placing her fork down, she indicated that she had finished and rose from her seat.

As Claire prepared to exit the room and head upstairs to bed to gather her thoughts for the upcoming Parliament meeting, a voice called, "Your Majesty, may I have a moment of your time?"

She turned, and her eyes landed upon Hans. *What did he want?* "Um, well, it's getting late, and I still have some business to attend to, so—"

He stood from his seat. "It won't take long, I promise."

She glanced at Ethan to ascertain his reaction.

His eyes darkened, and his jaw tightened.

Super. Not what she needed days before her wedding—Hans stirring up trouble. "I can spare a minute or two."

A smile spread across Hans' face, and he hurried around the table to join her. "Wonderful. Why don't we take a quick walk outside by the gardens? It's not dusk yet, and the warm summer evening air will feel nice."

"Okay, but again, I only have a few minutes." She led the way out of the room and toward the rear of the castle to the royal gardens. A house staffer opened the door for them, and Claire descended the steps to the pebbled pathway below. Waiting for Hans to join her, she tamped down her hands to keep from wringing them.

Once he fell in line behind her, the two walked down the path and away from the gathering.

After a few minutes, Claire broke the silence, "What is this about?" She glanced at him.

Hans brushed imaginary lint off his dinner jacket. "I wanted to see how things were progressing in your preparation for the Parliament meeting tomorrow. Are you prepared?"

Claire debated about how to answer him. She didn't want to give away too much, as she didn't trust him. Based on some of the items she'd uncovered, she wondered if he hadn't known about his father's plan all along. "I think so. I've looked over the financial books, and I have a good understanding of how the monarchy handled things in the past. Also, I've worked out a clear plan for the future. I hope that many of the discrepancies were simply misunderstandings that I can sort out in the coming months." Well, at least all of that held true—even if she hadn't shared how Maurelle had stolen money from her kingdom.

Hans stopped walking. "Good. Glad to hear it." He scooted closer and grabbed her cast-free hand in his. "Please know that if you need anything from me—" his eyes bore into hers, "anything at all, then I am here for you."

The sudden display of attention caused her to jolt and wrestle her hand away. She didn't want to make Hans uncomfortable but didn't dare encourage him. "Yes, well, I don't think that will be necessary, but thank you for your support." There—clear, concise, and detached. No way he or anyone else could mistake that for interest on her part.

"Wait." Hans took a step closer. "Hold still."

Claire froze but considered bolting for a second. *Where was this headed?* "Uh, I don't—"

Before she could finish quashing his advances, he raised a thumb to her cheek and brushed something away. "Sorry, you had an eyelash on your cheek." He took a step back.

Claire's shoulders relaxed. "Oh. Thanks."

The sun dipped near the horizon, casting a golden glow across the gardens. The hours had escaped Claire, and she didn't want to be caught out here with Hans alone after dark. Something told her that wouldn't go well—at all. "We should return to the castle. It's late, and I'm sure your father has missed you."

Hans gave a slight bow. He caught her eye as he straightened. "As you wish."

They took the footpath the rest of the way to the castle again without talking, but Claire's mind whizzed. Hans hadn't given up on his pursuit of her, but what were his intentions? Ethan wouldn't like it one bit, but she'd have to tell him. They had a policy—total honesty with one another.

Granny, of course, would love the intrigue of it all. Claire still had to reread her Parliament speech. Fatigue washed over her muscles as she climbed the rear castle stairs. All she wanted was to go to bed and cuddle with her dog. Maybe she could shelf the queen business for the night and wake up early in the morning to rehearse her speech.

Albert appeared at her side as she entered the rear castle door. "Your Majesty, it's rather late for a garden stroll, isn't it?"

"Yes, in fact, I believe I'll go to bed." She turned to address Hans. "Thank you for coming tonight. Please, give your father my regards as well." Then she focused on Albert once more. "Would you tell Ethan that this day has exhausted me, and I went to bed? Let him know that I'll call him first thing in the morning."

Albert bowed. "Very well, Your Majesty."

Claire hurried down the hallway and away from

Hans' prying eyes. At least she'd survived her encounter with him unscathed.

Chapter 15

Ethan watched as Hans reentered the Great Hall. He debated whether to engage him but didn't have long to consider the point.

Hans walked over to Ethan and extended his hand. "Good to see you again. I'm taking my leave for the night. It's proved to be a...valuable evening."

Ethan shook his hand and released it as quickly as possible. "Oh, really? Why is that?"

A self-assured smile spread across his face. "Well, I had a fascinating conversation with Queen Claire. She seemed rather enchanted with our walk. I told her if she ever needed my assistance," he lowered his voice, "with anything, then I'd be at her service."

Ethan could tell Hans' double-entendre meant more than to offer his help to the Crown as a fellow countryman, and he wanted to throw him out on his tail. "That won't be necessary. She's in capable hands between myself and her family. I should go home, too. I have the wedding in a few days if you recall."

Hans smirked. "We'll see." Then he turned on his

heel and sauntered away.

Fire rose from the pit of Ethan's stomach, and he wanted to chase down Hans and tackle him, but he decided that making the front page for a brouhaha wouldn't serve anyone well, least of all Claire. Ethan pulled in a deep breath, held it for a moment, and released it. It would be okay. Soon, he would watch his bride walk down the aisle to meet him, and he'd send Hans and his father home to Maltenstein and ship Maurelle off to an island or a castle or a jail far, far away. With that happy thought, he left the palace and headed home to get some rest. Tomorrow would look better.

~

A knock on the door startled Ethan, and he shot up from his bed like a rocket. He swiped away the sleep from his eyes. What was so crucial that someone had decided to give him a heart attack at seven in the morning?

The knocking on the door persisted, this time louder.

"I'm coming. Hold on," Ethan shouted, shrugging into a robe slung across a chair in his room before hurrying to the front door. He flung it open. "What?"

Michael stood at the door holding a newspaper in one hand and a hot tea in the other. His brow furrowed at the appearance of Ethan. "You were asleep? It's seven a.m. You're always up early. Does this mean you haven't seen the paper this morning?"

Ethan rubbed his face with his hand and then accepted the hot beverage his friend extended his way. "Yes, I was asleep. I had a long day yesterday, and it concluded with a less-than-cordial run-in with Hans Chicanery."

"Brace yourself then." Michael slapped the newspaper against Ethan's chest. "Because it doesn't look like the encounter has ended."

This assertion jolted Ethan to fully awake status, and he opened the paper to the front page. "No! This...She wouldn't...I can't—"

Michael stepped inside and headed into the living room, taking a seat in a chair. "Breathe. I'm sure it's not as bad as it looks. There must be an explanation."

Ethan's heart pounded in his chest. The front page of *The Amorley Tribune* depicted a picture of Claire and Hans standing close, and the position of Hans' head made it look like he'd leaned in for a kiss. "One explanation is that he kissed my fiancée!"

Michael nodded to the chair opposite his. "Sit down. Take a minute and hear what you're saying. Claire would never have let him kiss her. Even if he had, she didn't want him to do it because she's in love with you. She's marrying you. I'd say he caught her by surprise, and she didn't want to worry you with the story, or it's a misunderstanding."

Ethan's temple throbbed. Even if she hadn't encouraged Hans, the entire country would wake up to see this image with their morning coffee. It wouldn't do

Claire any favors with the public or Parliament. With the monarchy already under attack, he didn't know how many more onslaughts it could take. "This is the last thing she and I need right now. Claire has to speak in front of Parliament today about financial concerns and convince them that she isn't to blame and that the monarchy still has a useful role in Amorley's future. Oh, let's not forget the rehearsal dinner tomorrow night and the wedding the next day."

"It's going to work out. Find Claire. Talk to her. I'm sure she will make sense of it all. Leave Hans and his father to me. I have an idea."

"I can't forget about Maurelle, either. Who knows what sinister plot she's orchestrating?" Ethan flung the newspaper across the room.

"Let's confront one dragon at a time. Go to your fiancée. I'll deal with the Chicanery clan. We'll handle Maurelle when the time comes. Besides, after Claire's speech at Parliament today, won't Maurelle be finished?" Michael's eyebrows rose.

"All right. I'll go. Call me if you find out anything else, although I hope this is it for surprises for the day."

Chapter 16

Claire took the stairs two at a time and padded down the hallway to the dining room, anxious to start her day. A sliver of sunlight crept through the windows as if smiling on the reborn room after the fire. This would mark the first day of its use since that horrible event, and the thought made her grin. At least one good thing happened today.

At such an early hour, Claire expected to be the only one at the breakfast table, but the queen mother sat on one side near its head, peering intensely at a newspaper article, her reading glasses posted halfway down her nose.

"Good morning. How are you today?" Claire greeted her grandmother.

The queen mother lifted her head and shifted her gaze to Claire. Her eyes narrowed, and she removed her glasses. "How am I today? How am I?" She smacked the paper on the table. "I'm perplexed why you continue to find your way to the newspaper's front page based on scandal and ridicule of the Evercliff name."

The blood drained from Claire's head, and she froze. *What now? What could she have done this time?* "I don't know what you mean. How could they have reported anything new since the engagement dinner? You were here with me the entire time. Nothing crazy happened. At least I don't think it did."

"Well, I assure you something happened because a reporter got his hands on this." Her grandmother tossed the paper in Claire's direction and turned her head away. "Honestly, I thought by now I'd taught you something. You haven't learned anything—nothing at all."

Claire closed the gap between herself and her grandmother and lifted the paper from the table. Her eyes scanned the front page, then she gasped. "This looks horrible."

Her grandmother whipped her head around and glared at Claire. "I know. It's almost your wedding day. Today you have the Parliament address and the rehearsal dinner. This couldn't have happened at a worse time. I hope you have an explanation for that picture."

Claire's mouth went dry. "I—I went for a brief walk with Hans in the royal gardens, and he told me he would help me handle issues with his father. He did still seem interested in me, but I made it clear that I am in love with Ethan and that his advances were not welcome."

The queen mother pursed her lips. "If that is the

case, then how did you two come to appear so...cozy?"

Claire swallowed hard and thought back to the stroll. *The eyelash.* "This picture must have been taken when he brushed away a loose eyelash on my face. That's all that happened. It made me uncomfortable, but I told him that I needed to return to the castle, and that ended the conversation."

"Well, I can only imagine how Ethan must feel right now. Have you spoken with him?" The queen mother pushed up the glasses on the bridge of her nose.

Claire's stomach sank. "Oh no. Ethan. I'll go see him. He'll understand once I explain."

"Do you have time to go to his place before your address? Won't you be late? You still have to rehearse your speech and change clothes. Of course, you can't go before Parliament in that dress. You need to wear something smart. Why don't you call him?" the queen mother suggested.

"That's a great idea." Claire retrieved her phone from her skirt pocket and dialed Ethan's number. He didn't answer, and the call went to voicemail. At the sound of the beep, she blurted out an apology, "Ethan, I'm so sorry about the newspaper. Please call me when you get this. I can explain. I love you. Bye."

The queen mother shifted in her seat. She gave a slight nod. "There, you've called him. Now run along and get ready. You don't have any time to lose. If you can't convince Parliament and the Amorley people today that the monarchy has value and integrity, then we are finished."

Claire still yearned to speak to Ethan, to see his face. Leaving their relationship to the fate of a voicemail message sickened her. "Perhaps if I hurried, I could stop by his house or office on my way—"

Her grandmother raised a hand. "There's no time. You cannot be late for the address. Now, go. Get ready. Ethan will wait. You can speak to him later."

Claire nodded and left the room. She rehearsed her words for the umpteenth time and changed into a tea-length sapphire dress with a sweetheart neckline and patent-leather belt. Grabbing her bag, she hurried down the stairs, out the door, and into the waiting car.

Half an hour later, she exited the vehicle and stood in front of the Parliament building. Smoothing out her skirt, Claire took the steps slowly, careful not to fall.

Her security detail followed behind, and several photographers flanking the sides took pictures, calling for her to look their way.

She stared forward and lifted her head tall as her grandmother had taught her. *Don't fall. Don't trip.* Claire ascended the stairs and entered through the doors to her country's other seat of power. She swallowed hard. What if they didn't believe her? What if they still accused her of mismanagement or worse? She shook her head. No—stay positive. It will go well…it has to. Walking down the aisle, Claire passed by rows of Parliament members.

Some of them smiled and curtsied or bowed, but a

few maintained a stony expression and gave only the slightest nod of their head.

Yikes. Tough room. Claire took the steps to the platform at the front of the room and stood behind the empty podium. Afraid to bring the financial records she'd discovered in the book in the library for fear that they would get lost like her Coronation Day speech notes, she had forced herself to memorize the information. At least that was one thing she had total confidence in—her photographic memory. It had gotten her through medical school, and she prayed it would serve her well again today.

Claire stared at the packed room, and the rustling of papers and hum of murmuring ceased leaving a silent void for her to fill. Without thinking, she tapped the microphone attached to the podium to see if it worked.

It made three thuds with each pound of her fingertips and then squawked a warning that caused everyone in the room to cover their ears.

Super. Off to a great start. Clearing her throat, Claire began, "Ladies and gentlemen, fellow citizens, thank you for allowing me to speak to you today. It is a privilege to stand before you in the house of our lawmakers, and it is a responsibility and honor I do not take lightly. As your queen, I hold Amorley, its laws, and its people's welfare in high regard. When it came to my attention that there may have been financial mismanagement of the country's finances, I immediately took it upon myself to seek the truth."

The Parliament members murmured to one another, and several journalists jotted down her words in a frenzy.

Claire clasped her hands behind her back so no one could see them trembling. "As such, I believe that I have succeeded in this endeavor."

Everyone fell silent again.

Claire's palms began to sweat. She coughed to clear her throat. "It is true that there were unscrupulous acts with the management of Amorley's finances by the monarchy."

The crowd erupted in jeers. Shouts speckled with gasps, and more scribbling from the journalists and flashes from the press's cameras ensued.

Claire resisted the urge to shield her eyes from the blinding lights. *Stay the course. Deep breaths.* "It is true—however, I am not the responsible party. I have conclusive proof that my stepmother, Maurelle Evercliff, purposefully and willfully stole from the country's coffers and acted with the intent to conceal her crime. She used the country's money for her personal gain, above and beyond any reasonable amount approved by Parliament's allotment for her."

Maurelle, who stood near the front of the room, turned three shades of red and her complexion now verged on resembling an eggplant.

Several crowd members had turned their gaze upon Maurelle and started yelling insults and accusations in her direction.

Press onward. "Furthermore, I have additional evidence that indicates a plot between Maurelle and Lord Chicanery to use this financial blemish as a mark against my family and me to destroy the monarchy so that they may set up a new government, which they intend to control."

Shouts from the crowd drowned out the last bit of Claire's words, and it took several minutes for her to quiet them so she could respond. She raised a hand, palm forward. "Please, I am happy to answer questions. However, I can only answer one at a time."

The head of Parliament, Mr. Fulton, stood. "Your Majesty, with all due respect, may I ask where this evidence—this proof—is at present?"

Claire met his gaze. "Yes, of course. I have put the evidence, which includes a significant amount of paperwork and receipts, in a safe place so that it might not vanish. I will be happy to deliver it to you under secure guard this afternoon."

Another Parliament member rose from his chair. "How do we trust that you will carry the best interest of Amorley into the future? How can we be certain that something like this won't happen again?"

Claire smiled at the man. "I have attempted to become the perfect queen. However, I realized this week that I may not always meet such a standard. Sometimes, there will still be trips and falls, discordant microphone feedback, and even a toss or two off my horse. However, I pledge my allegiance to Amorley, its people, and its welfare before you today. Each day, I will strive to make our country stronger and better. My father left his legacy in my hands. By the grace of God, I plan to carry that legacy into the future."

The crowd jumped to its feet and erupted in a round of applause.

Heat warmed Claire's cheeks, and she gave the crowd a nod. Then, she scanned the room for Maurelle—except her stepmother had vanished. Hurrying down the platform stairs, Claire approached her head guard, John Rogers. "Have you seen my stepmother?"

He frowned and searched the room with his eyes. "No. Maurelle was just here."

Claire frowned. "As soon as we leave here, please send two of your guards to find her and retain her. This time, she's going to face her crimes."

The guard bowed. "Yes, Your Majesty."

Another flash from a photographer's camera reminded Claire of the newspaper picture earlier that day. *Ethan*. She had to find him. Hurrying through the room and exiting the Parliament building onto the street, she collided with him. "Oof. I'm so sorry. I was looking for you."

Ethan smiled at her, though tentative at first. "Me, too."

Claire pushed a loose strand of hair out of her eyes, tucking it behind her ear. "I want to explain about the newspaper picture. It—"

"It looked like you and Hans had become rather cozy." Ethan frowned.

Claire took Ethan's hand in hers, but he remained stiff. "It's not what it looked like at all. Remember when he asked to speak to me in the gardens?"

Ethan narrowed his gaze. "Yes," he replied, his voice even.

"Well, he set me up. I don't know how, but it's not the first time someone has orchestrated an unflattering picture of me without my knowledge." Claire squeezed his hand.

Ethan's shoulders relaxed. "That's true, but I told you not to trust him. I don't doubt that he would be interested in you—you're the Queen of Amorley, smart, and beautiful. He'd be insane not to pursue you, but I hoped you would have used better judgment."

Ethan's words stung. Claire dropped his hand. "What do you mean? Use better judgment—I don't see how it's my fault. He tricked me. I would have hoped that you would trust me as my fiancé and someone who knows me better than almost anyone else."

Grimacing, Ethan answered, "It's not about trust, but—"

"No, it is—don't you see? After everything—after all the trials with Maurelle, the coronation debacle, getting locked in the library secret room—you know me. You know I have integrity. Maybe not grace or poise, but I'm a person of my word, and my judgment is usually good." The more she considered the past few months' events, the angrier she became—not necessarily at Ethan but at the entire fiasco. She'd grown tired of fighting for the Crown.

Ethan's nostrils flared, and his jaw clenched. "Now, wait a moment. I can't believe you'd think I don't trust you. We're getting married tomorrow."

Tears filled Claire's eyes, and if she didn't get away from this conversation in the next few seconds, she would fall apart. "Are we? Everything is a mess. I have to deal with the catastrophe Maurelle created, and there'll probably be a trial. I doubt she'll confess. I'm trying to run a country and hold on to its trust by an inch. Wedding planning hasn't taken priority, and there are still a million things to do. I don't know, Ethan. I—"

Claire's head guard joined her and leaned close to her ear. "Your Majesty, we should go. I received word that there has been an incident at the castle."

"What's that?" Claire wrung her hands.

"It's urgent. I'd rather wait until we get in the car to say. There are too many reporters around, not that this news won't leak out soon." The guard resumed his upright, stoic position and waited for her to move to the awaiting car.

Claire glanced at Ethan, and all the hope she'd held for their bright future dissipated into the humidity hanging in the air. A fine drizzle began, and she shivered despite the summer heat. "I have to go."

Ethan raised a brow and hurt filled his eyes. "What

about us?"

"I can't think about anything else right now—I have to deal with Maurelle before she vanishes and find out what else has happened. I'm sorry." Claire turned away from her happy ending and ran to the car as fast as she deemed appropriate for a queen awaiting ruin.

As soon as she slid into the car, sobs wracked her body.

Her guard handed her a handkerchief before continuing, "It's bad news, I'm afraid. The worst, really."

"Well, don't let me sit here in suspense. This day has gone wrong already, so I can't imagine how much worse it could get."

The guard's lips narrowed into a firm, thin line. "Worse. There has been a fire at the castle."

Claire's eyes widened. "Another one? Is someone running around lighting matches and tossing them as they go?"

"It's quite serious, I'm afraid." The guard rubbed his jaw.

"Is everyone okay? Did everyone evacuate?" Claire asked.

The guard remained silent as the driver started the car's engine and hurried toward the castle.

Her throat tightened, and she squeaked out a thin, "No. Who?"

The guard pulled in a deep breath. "I'm not sure. All I know is that one person didn't escape. I haven't received any further information beyond that."

Granny? Wilson? No. "Hurry! Drive as fast as you can." She bowed her head onto her clasped hands and prayed with every ounce of fervor in her body, willing her loved ones to be okay. Please, God, let them just be okay.

Chapter 17

As the car pulled up to the castle, Claire's heart stopped. Speckling the entirety of Evercliff's driveway were multiple fire trucks, ambulances, and police cars. Most of the staff stood on the lawn looking bewildered.

"What?" She shook her head. "How did this happen?" she asked her head of security.

"I don't know, ma'am, but there's the fire chief near the front. Let's talk to him." He told the driver to stop the car and hopped out first, opening the door for Claire.

She quickly exited and ran across the lawn, shoving any pretense of royal etiquette aside. Claire yanked off her heels, held them in one hand, and burst across the yard at breakneck speed. Arriving at the fire chief's side, she gasped between breaths. "Please, tell me what is going on? How did the fire start? Is everyone okay? Did everyone make it out alive?"

To answer one of her questions, Wilson bounded up to her and licked her hand. "Hey buddy, it's so good to see you." She knelt and rubbed him behind his ears.

Leaning in, Claire kissed him on the head.

In return, he slurped her face with his velvet tongue.

For the first time that day, she chuckled. "You're a good boy." Claire gave him one final scratch on the head before rising. Then, she turned to the fire chief and waited for him to answer her barrage of questions.

He removed his helmet and wiped the sweat from his brow. Soot covered his face, and stress clouded his eyes. "As to the cause of the fire—I'm not sure, but I can tell you that it is suspicious. It doesn't look like an accident. Once they secure the area, my staff and the fire marshal will have to go through the scene. The official report will not be ready for weeks. However, I hope to have a preliminary idea of the cause by tomorrow. As soon as I know something definite, I'll let you know."

Claire shifted her weight and scanned the area, still not finding Granny. "What about the queen mother and my granny? I don't see them anywhere."

He pointed in the direction of a circle of firefighters centered around a single figure. "Your granny is over there holding court. She'll have them straightened out by the time she's done ordering my crew around." He smiled. "She's quite—"

Claire raised a brow and finished his thought for him. "Persistent? Bossy? Demanding?"

He laughed and raised both hands. "Hey, I didn't say it—you did. I'll give her this—she's a tough lady. I respect that."

Claire grinned. "I'm so thankful she's okay. What about the queen mother?"

He gestured across the lawn near one of the ambulances. "She's receiving treatment for smoke inhalation right now. It looks like she'll be fine, though."

Claire nodded. "I should check on her. I'll give Granny a few more minutes with the firefighters. She's in her element, I'm sure." She turned to leave, but the fire chief stopped her with the touch of his hand on her arm. "One more thing." He opened his mouth to speak but then closed it again.

Claire's brow furrowed. "What? What is it?"

"It's—it's about Albert, the head of the household." The fire chief ran a hand through his damp hair.

Claire froze at his name. "Go on."

He shifted his gaze and stared at his feet for a few seconds before continuing. "He...he didn't survive. Albert saved your granny and the queen mother but went back inside a third time to find the dog. He got him out but collapsed right afterward. Smoke inhalation or a heart attack is the most likely cause. The ambulance will take him to the medical examiner, and an autopsy may be performed, but I'd say that we know the cause. Still, he sacrificed his life with such bravery. None of them would be alive if it weren't for him."

Albert—her friend, confidant, and champion since

she'd arrived at the castle had died. He'd stood up for Wilson and helped Claire through many debacles. *How could he be gone?* Her throat ached, and tears filled her eyes. "No," she whispered. "No, it can't be true. It must be a mis...mistake. How could he...how could this have happened?" She clamped her trembling lips shut, unable to continue.

The fire chief tilted his head and sent her a pity-filled look. "I'm sorry, Your Majesty. I wish it weren't true. He was a hero. Is there anything else I can do?"

If Claire stood before him for one more second, she would fall apart. "No, thank you. I appreciate all that you've done. Now I'd better check on the queen mother." Before she left, she had another thought. "There is one more thing. Did you say what parts of the castle the fire damaged? Could you tell where the blaze started?"

The fire chief shifted his weight and grimaced. "Well, um, preliminarily—and this again is nothing official—it appears that the fire began in your bedroom and eventually engulfed that entire wing of the castle."

"The entire wing?" She shifted her eyes in the direction of that side of the castle. It didn't look different than usual except for the billows of smoke pouring out of the windows and swirling around the top of the building.

The fire chief nodded. "It doesn't look that impressive on the outside, but I assure you, the interior will need a total refurbishment. I'd say your bedroom and its contents are, unfortunately, a total loss."

Her bedroom held all of her journals, notes from her mother, mementos of her father, and proof of Maurelle's wrongdoing. Claire had tucked the financial papers away under her mattress—papers she'd planned to send via secure courier to the head of Parliament later today. Now, what would she do?

"Are you sure it's all gone?" She stared at him, praying he'd say this had all been a bad dream.

"I'm afraid so," he uttered.

Before she crumpled completely, she swallowed hard and gave a slight nod. "Right. Okay. Well, again, thank you for everything. Let me know the minute you determine the cause. I'll find the queen mother and see what else I can do to help. She and Albert had a close relationship. I'm sure she's beside herself."

He gave a slight bow and put his helmet back on his head before walking away.

Claire sprinted in the direction of the ambulances. Peeking inside each open door, she searched for her grandmother's face. On the third try, Claire found her. "Grandmother! I'm so thankful that you're okay." She ran to the older woman, forgetting all the royal lessons she'd been taught, and threw her arms around the queen mother's neck. "I'm so...I'm so sorry about Albert." Tears spilled down Claire's cheeks and her vision blurred.

The queen mother's disheveled, soot-stained blue skirt and blazer looked equally as uncharacteristic as the bewildered expression on her face. "I don't know what happened. One minute I sat in my bedroom having a cup of tea and reading a book, and the next thing I knew, smoke filled the hallway. Before long, I couldn't see anything. Albert rushed in and carried me to safety."

"What a wonderful, brave man," Claire blubbered. She released her grandmother and rubbed the moisture from her cheeks with the back of her hand.

Tears pooled in her grandmother's eyes, but to her credit, she maintained her composure otherwise. "Yes, he was indeed."

"The chief said the fire started in my bedroom—or at least that's what they think. If I caused this fire and Albert's death—if I left something on or somehow made this happen—I—I don't think I could live with..." She sniffled and swallowed again, willing herself not to fall to the ground in a weepy puddle.

Her grandmother placed a gentle hand on Claire's cheek. "I'm sure it's not your fault. The castle's electrical wiring is old, and the castle is even older. These things happen. We'll rebuild. Try not to feel guilty."

Claire couldn't help but think if she'd stayed in Boston, she'd have saved everyone a lot of trouble. Everything was ruined now—Albert, her wedding reception, her defense to Parliament, Ethan. She shook her head. Who would have thought that the unflattering photo with Hans would be the best thing that happened today?

The drizzle that had started early in the morning turned to large droplets and pelted her face. She winced. *Perfect.* She'd drown in tears and rain if she didn't get out of here. Claire looked at her grandmother. "I'm glad you're safe, but I need...I need to check on something. I'll be right back."

The queen mother nodded as if she understood that Claire didn't want to fall to pieces in front of her. "Go."

Claire took off at a fast walk which quickly transitioned to a light jog and then a full-out run in the lake's direction. By the time she arrived at the water's edge, the rain had turned into thick sheets, and her clothing stuck to her skin. She dropped to the ground and wept.

How could this have happened? Every time happiness was within her grasp, something terrible occurred and yanked it away. She'd nearly missed being named the future heir to the Amorley throne. Then she'd almost blown her coronation speech after Maurelle stole her notes. Now the fire had destroyed Claire's only proof that she was innocent of mishandling Amorley's finances. The future of her role as queen of Amorley didn't look bright—not to mention that she'd lost a true friend with Albert's death.

At that moment, a familiar male voice called from behind her, "Oh, I'm so thankful that you are all right."

Ethan.

Claire raised her brow. "Ethan, you're here. But

how did you know about the fire?"

"After you left me in front of Parliament, Michael called. His cousin works for the fire department. When he heard the address for the call, he let me know. If I'd lost you, I—" his voice broke.

Claire blinked hard and then stared out across the lake. "I'm fine...but Albert...." She couldn't finish the thought.

Ethan knelt next to her. "I know. I heard. I'm sorry, Claire—not just about Albert but about everything. I'm sorry that we fought, that I let a silly picture affect me like that. Of course, I trust you. I love you. We've been down this road too many times before. I want to marry you, and I'm not letting anything stand in the way of that." He placed his hand under her chin and tilted it toward his face. "Will you forgive me for doubting you?"

Tears swam in front of her eyes, and she blinked hard. No matter what else happened, she had Ethan. He loved her. "Of course, I do. Are you sure you still want to marry me? You're aligning yourself with a mess—I lost the proof that I had no involvement in the financial wrongdoing in the fire. So stupid—I hid it under my mattress, and the blaze destroyed that entire wing of the castle. Now it's my word against Maurelle's."

He brushed her tears away with his thumb and smiled. "You're not a mess—you're perfect."

Claire sniffled. "Ha. That's funny. I'm far from that."

"Okay, maybe not perfect; no one is perfect. God made you perfectly in His image, and that's what counts. We can't control everything, but you're right about one thing—I do want to align myself with you forever. I can't wait until tomorrow comes to make you my bride." He leaned closer and pressed his warm lips against hers, kissing away her hurt and pain.

When they parted, fresh tears fell down her face, and Claire rubbed them away with the back of her hand. "I still can't believe Albert's gone. He helped me, and I trusted him. Did the fire chief tell you that Albert saved Granny and the queen mother—oh, and Wilson?" Her shoulders heaved at the thought of losing one of her greatest champions.

Ethan stroked her hair and whispered, "I'm sorry." Then, he fell silent and let her cry.

She poured out all the anguish and frustration of the past weeks—no, the past months—until nothing remained. Once her sobbing subsided to a sputtering whimper, she sucked in a long, deep breath and exhaled. "Okay. Enough of this. I can't sit here all day staring at the lake, crying. If I'm going to save my father's legacy and Amorley's future, I need to pull myself together and ask God to help me."

Ethan nodded and squeezed her shoulder. "Could I pray for you?"

She nearly lost it again but fought to maintain the composure she'd regained. In a low voice, she agreed, "That would be great. Thank you."

Ethan rested his forehead against hers and nestled close, taking her hand in his. "Father, thank you for the gift of loyal friends like Albert. I pray that you will renew Claire's strength as she's going through this dark time and carry her forward in the power of your peace. Show her how to save Amorley and heal her heart from this great loss of a friend and confidant. Thank you for keeping the rest of her family safe and blessing us with one another. Show her what to do next. Amen." He raised his head and opened his eyes, sending her a grin. "I love you."

She smiled and sighed. "I love you, too. I—"

Loud barking interrupted her, and Wilson galloped across the lawn, heading straight towards her. It looked like he had something in his mouth. *Please don't let it be a dead animal.* She didn't think she could cope with one more thing today.

The rambunctious dog nearly knocked her over with his arrival, wagging his tail in excitement.

Claire scratched behind his ear and leaned forward to give him a quick kiss on his head. "It's good to see you, too, buddy. What do you have there?" She squinted, trying to determine what treasure he'd brought her this time. It looked like a mass of crumpled papers. "Drop it," she commanded and waited to see if he'd choose to listen this time. Usually, she had a fifty-percent chance of him complying with her request.

Wilson dropped the papers to the ground and sat on his hindquarters, wagging his tail. His tongue hung out, and he smiled, looking particularly pleased with himself at his find.

Claire picked up the damp papers and unfolded them. "Wilson, honestly, this is so gross. Why do you have to drag in everything you find and—" She gasped.

Ethan's head shot upward, and he raised a brow. "What? What is it?"

Claire's mouth dropped open as she scanned the first page. "Do you know what this is?"

Ethan shook his head. "What?" he asked again.

"This is the proof of Maurelle's wrongdoing. Somehow—and I don't know how—Wilson must have found the papers in my bedroom and carried them outside. I can't imagine how he didn't ruin them in the process or lose them, but—" Claire flipped through the papers quickly to see if they were all there, "he brought every single page."

Ethan grinned. "That's a miracle."

A smile tugged at the corners of her lips. "It's more than that. It's an answered prayer." She carefully folded the papers in half again and tucked them under one arm. Then, Claire scooped Wilson into a hug, facing him again. "You are the best boy in the whole world. What a good, good boy." She rubbed his head with her free hand, and happy tears filled her eyes. Maybe everything would work out. Perhaps she'd save Amorley and her father's legacy from Maurelle's latest attack, and she'd walk down the aisle tomorrow and marry Ethan. Claire would have her happily ever after—regardless of how imperfect it might be, soot-covered and all.

Ethan rose from his spot and reached his hand to her. "Come on. We have a lot to do if you're going to have your perfect wedding tomorrow and rescue Amorley."

Claire took his hand and stood.

He pulled her close to his chest and kissed her forehead.

She stared into his kind blue eyes, and her breath caught in her throat for a moment. "I don't need a perfect wedding."

He raised a brow. "No?"

Claire ran her fingers along Ethan's jaw. "No," she whispered.

He searched her face with his eyes. "What do you need then?"

She smiled and tilted her head. The wind blew and carried the fragrance of honeysuckle intermingled with the scent of Ethan's musk, and Claire's pulse quickened. "You. I just need you." Then, she lifted her head toward his, closed her eyes, and melted into his lips. For one last moment, Claire allowed herself a bit of bliss before she picked up her paper sword to fight the dragon.

Chapter 18

Ethan walked with Claire to the front of the castle. The firefighters had extinguished the blaze, though billows of dark smoke circled above the east wing. It would be a long time before the Evercliff returned to its original glory—much longer than the candlestick debacle.

Claire grabbed his arm. "There's Granny. I'm going to tell her the good news about the financial paperwork and make sure she and Grandmother are okay. Maybe you should head home and get some rest. We have a big day tomorrow."

Lines appeared on his forehead. "And leave you here alone to deal with this mess? You would have to go to the head of Parliament alone. Not possible. I'm here for the duration."

She sent him a relieved smile. "Thanks. Okay, give me a second to check in with them, and then we'll call the head of Parliament, Mr. Fulton, and let him know I'm delivering the proof."

He nodded. "While you do that, I'll talk with the

fire chief and find out if and when we can use the unaffected part of the castle or if we need to find a hotel for everyone."

Claire rubbed her head. "I hadn't even considered that they might not let us use the castle. Wonder where we'll have the wedding reception now? The ballroom is probably toast—literally."

Ethan turned to leave but stopped. "What about Albert's family? Is there anyone we need to notify?"

Another wave of tears filled Claire's red-rimmed eyes. "I—I don't believe he had any extended family. No wife, no kids. We were his family."

Rubbing Claire's arms, he frowned. "I'm sorry. I didn't realize."

She shook her head and sniffled. "It's okay. You couldn't have known."

He gave her a final squeeze and kissed the top of her head. "Go talk to Granny. No matter how tough life gets, she always has wise words and makes you laugh. Let me know when we need to leave to meet Mr. Fulton."

"All right." Claire glanced down at her soot-covered clothing. Not perfect, but it didn't matter. She hurried away to find Granny and the queen mother.

~

Renewed with fresh determination, Ethan got to work. He waited for the chief to finish a conversation with one of the Evercliff waitstaff before asking for an update. As the waitstaff walked away, Ethan stepped forward. "I realize you're busy, but Queen Claire wanted me to find out if Evercliff's residents will be able to return to the castle tonight? We weren't sure if it would be closed for a time or if the unaffected wing would be safe for the staff and royal family to return to this evening. It's getting late, and I'm certain everyone is tired."

The fire chief removed his hat and tucked it under an arm, wiping his brow with a handkerchief. He stuffed the cloth in his pocket. "I spoke with my staff, and they contained the fire to the east wing. Therefore, the other side of the castle should be habitable. However, the ballroom won't be usable for the next month. There doesn't appear to be structural damage there, but the smell of smoke is too strong. I thought my wife told me that you two were holding the wedding reception there. If so, you will have to find somewhere else."

Ethan frowned. "That's not what I wanted to hear, but I understand. I'll inform Claire. In the meantime, is it all right if I send the staff and residents in now?"

The fire chief glanced at the castle. "I don't see why not but tell everyone that they must stay away from the east wing. I'll have my men cordon off the damaged area. Tell your people not to explore the affected zone—it's not safe. I'll file my report in the morning with the fire marshal, and hopefully, he'll have his formal assessment ready in a few days. Then, you can begin the clean-up process." The fire chief turned to leave but paused with a tired smile. "Oh, and congratulations on the upcoming wedding."

Ethan lifted a hand and waved. "Thank you." Then, he watched as the fire chief walked away. Smoke burned Ethan's eyes, and fatigue had started to set in from the intensity of the day. His eyelids grew heavy, but he rubbed them, willing himself to press onward. He still had a lot to do. First, he called the head of Parliament and made a plan to meet with him and Claire in a few hours.

Time passed quickly as Ethan busied himself with assisting everyone into the safe part of the castle and ensuring that they had a room to sleep in for the night. Once the front lawn had cleared, and the fire trucks, ambulances, and police cars had pulled away, Ethan hurried to find his fiancée standing with Granny. "Claire, we should go if we're going to make it to our appointment with the head of Parliament."

She nodded and turned to Granny. "Are you sure you're all right? Do you need me to stay with you?"

Granny swatted Claire's arm. "Get out of here. Save the world—or at least Amorley. I'm fine. How many times do I have to tell you what a tough old bird I am? Besides, it's me who should be asking if you're okay. Losing Albert is—" her voice broke for a second, "well, it's hard."

Claire hugged her granny and inhaled the comforting scent of lavender from her granny's perfume despite the bitter smell of smoke. She exhaled and released her. "It is hard, but we have to press on for his sake. He wouldn't want Maurelle and the Hans brigade to win."

Granny smirked. "My thoughts exactly. No, you go, and I'll stay here to keep everyone in line. I'll watch Wilson, too."

Leave it to Granny to think about Wilson. Most nights, he slept with Claire, but in the evening before bedtime, he would often run the castle halls with Albert, following him around as if Albert were his master. Her furry friend would miss Albert as much as she would. "Thanks." She kissed her granny on the cheek and turned to Ethan. "Let's win back the castle."

Chapter 19

Claire couldn't stop wringing her hands in her lap as the car pulled up to the head of Parliament's home. She and Mr. Fulton hadn't always gotten along well, but recently, things had improved.

Ethan reached across the seat and squeezed Claire's hand. "You can do this."

She nodded but remained silent, rehearsing in her mind the words she'd practiced several times before.

The driver stopped the car and exited, opening her door and waiting while she stepped out of it.

Glancing at Ethan, Claire sent him a smile. "Thank you."

Ethan started to slide out of the car, but Claire placed a gentle hand on his arm. "Do you mind waiting here? This is something I have to do on my own." At least she thought so.

His brow lifted, and he asked, "Are you certain?" His clipped accent still caused her pulse to race.

"I'm positive. This time, I must face my dragons on my own, but there is something you can do."

His face broke into a wide grin. "Anything you wish, my queen."

Heat rose from her chest and filled her neck and face. "Would you pray for me while I'm inside?"

Ethan smiled. "Of course. Consider prayers lifted." Then, he took her hand and brought it to his soft lips, kissing it gently while gazing down at her. He released her hand and dipped his head. "Go slay away."

She sent him a nervous smile and turned to face the head of Parliament's house. The twenty or so steps between her car and the front door felt like crossing an ocean. When she arrived at his front door, she raised her hand to knock and paused. *What if he doesn't believe her documentation? What if Maurelle wins?* Claire's father's legacy would be lost forever.

Granny's words of encouragement echoed in her mind, and she considered how one day she wanted to call herself a tough old bird, too, so she pulled herself together, took a deep breath, and knocked on the door.

Mr. Fulton opened the door, worry lines framing his forehead and his eyes. "Your Majesty, please come inside. I hope you have good news for me. While we may not always agree on all matters, I can't say I look forward to the unrest that would come from your stepmother's or Lord Chicanery's leadership." He held the door open further and gestured for her to enter, bowing as she passed him.

Once inside, Claire followed him down the hallway and into his study.

He stood behind his seat. "I'm surprised that your security detail isn't on your heels."

She shrugged. "Well, with all the chaos at the castle right now, I told them they could send one guard with me, and I may have bribed him with coffee and pastry on the way home if he agreed to wait in the car. It was no easy feat."

Mr. Fulton smiled. "That seems like a small price to pay for one's freedom."

"Agreed." Claire shifted her weight and fiddled with a smudge of soot on the edge of her sleeve.

He pointed toward another empty chair in his study. "Please, take a seat. May I bring you anything? Tea? Coffee? I heard about the fire. You probably haven't had time to eat dinner. My apologies about the castle. It's a terrible business."

After she sat down, he followed suit. She waved away his offer of food and drink. "No, thank you. I couldn't eat anything right now. As you said, it's a stressful time, and the last thing on my mind is food. If you hadn't heard, my head of the household, Albert, passed away. He died saving the queen mother and my granny."

The head of Parliament's shoulders sagged, and genuine pity crossed his face. His voice softened. "I'm sorry. That must be so upsetting. I've met him on several occasions, and he was a solid gentleman—very professional."

Claire nodded. "It's a tragic loss. The fire chief and

fire marshal are investigating the blaze. They have concerns that someone intentionally set it, but they haven't confirmed anything yet."

He gasped. "How awful. Do they have any suspects?"

Claire debated about revealing her working diagnosis of the most likely culprits but decided instead to keep her opinions to herself. "Not yet, but the fire chief said it would take time to get to the bottom of it. However, that's not why I'm here."

He sat back in his chair and straightened his posture. "Right. Absolutely. Please, proceed."

Chewing on her bottom lip, Claire considered running down the hallway, out the door, and onto the next plane to Boston. Instead, she swallowed hard and plowed ahead. "As I said earlier today, I have proof—conclusive proof, mind you—of wrongdoing by the former queen and my stepmother, Maurelle Evercliff."

He frowned and leaned forward. "That's a serious accusation. Are you certain?"

Claire's hands trembled as she withdrew the financial paperwork from within the large leather tote that she'd brought with her. "I am. As I reviewed the entries in the public accounting record that you'd given me and investigated the discrepancies between the record and the balance sheet, I found, as you did, items that indicated withdrawals from the monarchy via the Amorley Care Fund."

He steepled his fingers together and rested his chin

on the tips of his fingers. "Yes, but this is not new information."

Clearing her throat, Claire flipped through the papers she'd brought with her until she found one of the pages where she'd circled with a red pen an entry that held initials and a scribbled note about the reason for the withdrawal. "Right. However, while in the Evercliff library, I discovered an old book that held what appeared to be a second set of accounting forms. Another set of financial books, if you will. The entries in this one paint a clearer picture of where each concerning item in the first set of papers went. This one has the same amount of money removed, the person's initials who requested the funds, and a small note about the real reason for the withdrawal."

Mr. Fulton's brow furrowed further. "Really? Whose initials and handwriting did you find?"

Claire pointed to the first entry on the page and scooted her chair closer to Mr. Fulton so that he could see it, too. "Here. Take a look at the initials."

Mr. Fulton lifted a pair of reader glasses from the side table next to his chair. He placed them atop his nose and peered at the handwriting. "I don't see how that is conclusive proof, Your Majesty. I'd assume several people in the world could have the same initials."

Tapping the paper, Claire insisted, "Yes, but look here and compare it to this note I received for my coronation. It's from my stepmother, given to me as a congratulatory message." Clare forced herself to withhold a withering expression and remain impassive. "The handwriting matches."

He narrowed his eyes and inspected the note and the financial ledger entry. "So, it does. Why would Maurelle do this?"

Claire shuffled the papers in her lap into a neat stack again. "I can explain that, too. She always wanted to rule. As my father's wife, my stepmother planned to take the throne as queen forever, or at least for the foreseeable future. With his death, and my right to the Crown uncovered, she faced losing that power. I found a letter between her and Lord Chicanery. It appears they formulated a plot to make the monarchy appear untrustworthy and useless, so they could put forth the concept of creating a new democracy in Amorley. Of course, they planned to rule this government themselves and marry to join Chicanery's country with Amorley. He would obtain Amorley's wealth, and Maurelle would double her power. I believe she hoped that if a financial scandal came to light, I would slink away and not put up much of a fight. But she was wrong. I've been through too much to let this country and my father's legacy fall into selfish, unworthy hands." She closed her mouth and caught her breath.

"Well, that was quite a speech. May I?" He raised a brow and reached out a hand, waiting for her to hand him the remainder of the paperwork.

She passed the forms over to him. "Of course."

Claire sat in silence while Mr. Fulton perused the sheets.

Thirty minutes later, he lifted his head and removed his glasses, placing them back on the side table again. "This paperwork looks authentic and fairly condemning for your stepmother, but I'll have to discuss it with the authorities to validate everything. However—" he rubbed the bridge of his nose and closed his eyes, "I see no evidence of wrongdoing on your or your father's part. Therefore, I will make a motion in the morning to place a vote of confidence in you and your leadership and send with you my prayers and blessings for a happy wedding tomorrow."

Claire exhaled, and tears filled her eyes. "Oh, thank you, thank you, thank you." She lunged across the space and flung her arms around the head of Parliament's neck. According to her grandmother, such an outpouring of emotion was not queen-like, but she didn't care.

"Oof." He tensed.

When Claire released him, she regained her composure. "Sorry about that, but seriously thank you so much for listening to me and believing my story."

He sent her a small smile. "Despite what you might think, I am rooting for you, as the expression goes. You will make a great queen."

Claire gathered her tote and rose from her chair. "Should I leave the papers with you? I hate to let them out of my sight, but I imagine you'll need them to present to the authorities."

He nodded. "I will need them, but I assure you that I will take care of them." Mr. Fulton stood from his seat.

She nodded and followed Mr. Fulton down the hallway and to the front door. Claire floated across his lawn to the driveway where her car and Ethan waited. Turning around before she slid into the vehicle, she tossed a wave to the head of Parliament, the way her grandmother had taught her.

Mr. Fulton bowed.

Claire's driver opened the door for her, and she slid inside the car.

Ethan turned to face her. "Well? What did he say?"

Claire grinned. "He said that we should get hitched. I have slain a dragon."

He broke into a wide smile. "That's great news. I knew you could do it." He scooped her into his arms and planted a deep kiss on her lips. When he released her, he whispered, "Let's go home, my fierce, strong Queen Claire. We have a wedding to attend."

Her eyes settled on his, and a slow smile tugged at her lips. "Yes, we do."

Ethan offered a hand to her as the car's engine roared to life. She placed her hand in his and gave it a squeeze. As she did, her hopes rose. Perhaps she'd have her happily ever after.

Chapter 20

A commotion sounded from downstairs, awakening Claire from a horrid dream. During the nightmare, she had gotten lost in a forest, rain pouring down on her head. Every time she followed what appeared to be the right path, she ended up at the same tree.

Voices from the entryway bellowed, but her room stood far enough away that she couldn't understand them. She sat up in bed, rubbed the sleep from her eyes, and shivered. That dream had been too realistic—it wasn't long ago when she'd found herself lost in the Dark Forest after an ill-fated outing with Maurelle. Lately, her entire life had felt like that trip in the woods—uncertain, lonely, and scary at times. Fortunately, with Ethan's reassurances, she'd gone to sleep last night feeling better about the wedding and Mr. Fulton's affirmation about the monarchy. Still, Maurelle had a way of upending circumstances.

"I cannot believe this. I won't stand for it. Get your hands off of me!" Claire's stepmother's shrill voice echoed from the first floor.

Claire jumped out of bed and grabbed her robe off the corner chair of her bedroom. It wasn't queenly to pad downstairs in her pajamas and slippers, but she had no time to change. Something major had happened, but she refused to let Maurelle ruin her wedding day. Claire had to defend herself.

Arriving at the bottom of the stairs, Claire stopped. Maurelle stood in the doorway encircled by four police officers. One of them had secured Maurelle's arms behind her back in handcuffs. Her stepmother's face had turned a deep crimson color, and her raven hair jutted out wildly in every direction.

Claire's jaw dropped. "What is going on?"

The police officer near the front of the group who appeared to be in charge, stepped forward. He removed his hat and bowed. "I'm Officer Peterson, Your Majesty. I apologize for the intrusion, especially on your wedding day, but this matter couldn't wait."

Claire tightened her robe closer to her body. "What matter is that?"

Officer Peterson tucked his hat under his arm and met her eyes. "The matter of Amorley vs. Queen Maurelle Evercliff. Parliament issued a complaint to the authorities late last night about a plot to overthrow Your Majesty as well as significant proof of embezzlement of government funds. We received an urgent warrant for her arrest for treason. I am here to arrest Maurelle Evercliff and take her into custody."

Granny's voice cackled from behind Claire, "You mean she's going to the slammer? Woo-hoo—I couldn't have planned it better myself. I can't wait to see what she looks like in those striped jumpsuits."

Whipping her head around, Claire glared at her granny. "That is not helpful."

The pure glee on her granny's face almost caused Claire to snicker, but she bit her lower lip to compose herself. After all, her stepmother hadn't exactly endeared herself to Claire—leaving her stranded in the woods at nightfall, locking her in a tomb-like study, sending her on a runaway horse, and almost ruining the coronation. Still, her mother's words swam through Claire's mind always to be kind to others. Always.

She sighed. "Officer, can you explain to us what happens next? Also, I assume you know that she did not act alone in this alleged series of events."

He nodded. "Oh, we are fully aware of that, Your Majesty. Another squadron went to collect her fellow conspirators, Hans Chicanery and his father, Lord Edward Smythe Chicanery, from their chambers. Unfortunately, the officers found empty beds and a note stating that they had left the premises for a prior engagement."

Claire snorted. "A prior engagement—right."

The officer sent her an empathetic grin. "Don't worry, we will find them."

Rubbing her forehead, Claire sighed. Why couldn't anything be simple in her life? "Do you think they are dangerous? Should we postpone the wedding?"

The officer shook his head. "Leave it to me. Enjoy your wedding day. We will find the missing offenders, and I am delivering Queen Maurelle to the precinct myself."

Claire nodded. "Thank you." Then, her eyes shifted to Maurelle.

Her stepmother wore a sneer, and she pulled against the restraint of the officer holding her arms. "You must love this—you will be married and seal your position as the queen of a country you stole from me."

Stepping forward, Claire closed the distance between herself and Maurelle. "I feel sorry for you."

Maurelle's eyes flashed. "Why is that?"

"Because you've never known true love—God's love. If you had, you would know that there's more to life than position and power. Ruling Amorley isn't about being in charge—it's about serving the people— humbling oneself. My marriage isn't a way to secure my spot on the throne. It's a ceremony uniting two people in love under God's banner."

Maurelle rolled her eyes. "Please."

Claire tilted her head. "I pray that you open your heart, Maurelle, to God, to love, to others. Not everything in life is a battle. Not everything is a competition."

Her stepmother glared. "You don't know anything. This isn't the last you've heard from me."

Claire stared at Maurelle for a moment, and her

heart sank. Only God could soften her heart to see the wrongful acts she'd committed. Glancing at Officer Peterson again, she took a step backward. "Thank you again for your help."

The officer bent at the waist once more and put on his hat. "My pleasure, Your Majesty." Then, he gave a nod toward the officers managing Maurelle. Once the officers and Maurelle had left through the castle's front entrance, one of the waitstaff closed the door with a thud.

"Well, good riddance," Granny chortled.

"I should feel happy it's over—that I have proven my innocence, secured the monarchy, and brought Maurelle's true intentions to light—but I'm sad."

Granny frowned and walked over to Claire. "Why's that, my dear? That woman was a snake if I ever saw one. She tried to kill you more than once."

"It just seems like a waste of a life—to carry around so much hate and anger like that. Something about it makes me sorrowful for her. That her heart is that cold."

"She's not totally cold." Granny pointed with her finger. "She likes those horses, but that's about it."

Claire shook her head. "You're a mess. Thanks for being here with me. I wouldn't have made it to this day without you." Tears pooled in her eyes as the last few weeks' events flashed through her mind.

Granny patted her on the back. "I love you. I'm always here to jump in the trenches with you, but why the tears? Wedding-day jitters?" She raised a brow.

Claire brushed away a tear from her cheek. "I wish Albert were here. It's silly, I only knew him for a little while, but he became family. Having him in the castle made me feel like I had an insider rooting for me."

Granny hugged her. "He would be proud of how far you've come." She released Claire and wiped away the remainder of her granddaughter's tears. "Now, let's get you married."

Claire grinned. "Okay. Thanks, Granny."

Granny winked at her. "Anytime."

~

Standing before the full-length mirror in her bedroom, Claire stared at the image before her—a confident young woman wearing a white lace-covered, mermaid-silhouetted gown and a shimmering tiara. She twisted her engagement ring on her fourth finger with her thumb and let her eyes wander down to the stone. Married—she, Dr. Claire Thomson—was getting married. Somehow, her wedding day felt more surreal than being crowned queen of Amorley.

She smiled as she thought about Ethan. He loved her, and she adored him. Despite having thwarted Maurelle's efforts to destroy her happiness, Claire knew life would bring more hurdles in the future. Still, when those dragons had to be slain, Claire wouldn't want to do it with anyone other than Ethan.

Smoothing her gown one last time, she drew in a deep breath.

A knock on her bedroom door pulled her out of her reverie.

Claire glanced at her reflection once more. "Come in."

Her grandmother opened the door and entered the bedroom. "I wanted a word with you before we have to leave for the church."

Sweat dampened the back of Claire's neck. What had she done now? Oh, wait, let's see—over the past few weeks, she'd almost burned down the castle, nearly lost the Crown to Maurelle, and watched one of her great confidants, Albert, pass away. None of those things were directly Claire's fault, but still. "Of course. What's on your mind?"

Crossing the room, her grandmother caught Claire's eye. Her stoic face broke into a wide grin. She uncharacteristically scooped her granddaughter into an embrace and squeezed her. After a few seconds, she gave Claire an awkward pat on the back before releasing her. "You look lovely. Enchanting."

"Thank you. You look nice, too." Claire nodded toward the queen mother's wedding attire of a designer blush-toned skirt and blazer.

The queen mother bristled, appearing uncomfortable with the praise, but replied, "Yes, Mademoiselle Couture outdid herself, but that's not what I wanted to discuss with you."

Claire swallowed. *Here it comes.* "What did I do now?"

The queen mother raised a brow. "What makes you think you've done something wrong?"

She shrugged and chuckled. "It usually is the case—or if it's not me, it's Wilson or Granny."

Her grandmother suppressed a smile, but her eyes sparkled. "I won't argue with that point, especially about that dog of yours; however, this time, I want to give you praise."

Claire's shoulders relaxed. There would be no speeches about poise today. "For what?" she asked.

"It is my opinion that you have handled yourself with grace and integrity. Facing the difficult situation of balancing your career, this country's needs, your fiancé, and fending off attacks on the Crown, you have remained steadfast. You proved your innocence. You stood up to Maurelle and her hoodlums and handled the fire, the loss of a friend and loyal attendant, and so many other unexpected obstacles with grace and poise. I'm impressed, and your father would be, too. He'd tell you that aside from making a most beautiful bride today, you have made him proud and will lead Amorley into a bright future."

Now Claire launched into full-on blubbering mode. So much for grace and poise.

Her grandmother produced a handkerchief from her pocket.

Claire took it and noticed it had the queen mother's initials embroidered on it. Of course, it did—her grandmother paid attention to details like that. She sniffled and dabbed her eyes. "Thank you. That means a lot to me."

The queen mother gave a slight nod, then pursed her lips, back to business. "Yes, well, that's enough of that, I suppose. We must get to the abbey, or your fiancé will think you've gotten—what is it you say in America? Cold feet?"

Claire laughed and wiped away one last tear. "You've nailed it—cold feet. Yes, I wouldn't want to cause Ethan any further distress. I'd say he's been through enough over the past few months."

"Very well." Her grandmother pivoted and walked out the bedroom door.

Claire followed behind her, wondering what her mother would have said about her only daughter's wedding day. Giving her ring a final glance, Claire smiled. Mona Thomson would have been happy for Claire; she was sure of it. That happy thought washed away all the horribleness of the past days.

Descending the stairs, Claire whispered a prayer of thankfulness for the love of a wonderful man and the new family she'd formed here at Evercliff. Royal or not, she felt loved, and that was all anyone could ask for.

Chapter 21

Ethan tugged at his bowtie for the umpteenth time and loosened it.

Michael grimaced and took a step forward. He reached for the bowtie, whacking his friend's hands away. "Would you let me do that? For a noble, you're terrible at this."

Frowning, Ethan stood still and let Michael help him. "Thanks a lot," his voice dripped with sarcasm.

Two seconds later, Michael had whipped the bowtie into a respectable knot, and he stood back, inspecting his work. "Perfect, if I do say so myself."

Ethan snorted.

Michael feigned offense. "Is that any way to treat your best mate?"

Considering all the pair had endured over the past few weeks, Ethan became serious. "I don't know how to thank you for all you've done. If it hadn't been for you, not only would Claire have never made it to her coronation, but we probably wouldn't be getting married today. I don't want to think about what would have happened to Amorley if you hadn't helped uncover Maurelle's plot. Maybe I should ask Claire to give you a knighthood."

Michael stroked his chin with his hand. "Hmm, a knight, you say. Sir Michael—I like the sound of that." He held his head higher and straightened his shoulders.

Ethan shook his head. "Oh no, I've created a monster. If it's going to go straight to your head, consider the knighthood off." He gave his friend a gentle slug on the arm.

Raising his hands, Michael conceded, "All right, I'll keep things in perspective. Perhaps, I'll only use my formal title at royal events." He chuckled.

Ethan smiled. "Very humble of you." He turned and inspected himself in the mirror—his wedding day. There were recent moments when he doubted this day would ever come, but he and Claire had made it here together despite all the adversity. He couldn't wait to marry her and make her his wife.

"You're grinning like a fool in love." Michael tightened his own bowtie and tugged on his tuxedo jacket.

Ethan buttoned his jacket and turned to face his best friend. "That's because I am one."

Michael smiled. "I'm happy for you and Claire. May you both live a long and blissful life—and make me a knight." He laughed.

Rolling his eyes, Ethan waved for Michael to follow him. "Let's go. I don't want to leave my bride waiting for me at the altar. Plus, I would never put it beyond Maurelle's capabilities to devise a last-minute evil plot, even from prison." Ethan opened the door and walked outside.

Michael followed behind. "Hmm. You have a point. Let's get you to the church."

The two friends hurried to the limousine waiting for them and took their places in the back seat.

Ethan's palms began to sweat, but all his fears and worries disappeared when he closed his eyes and imagined Claire's beautiful face. Today he would marry the love of his life.

Chapter 22

Claire stared out of the horse-drawn carriage and swallowed hard. Today was it—her wedding day. Somehow against all odds, she and Ethan had made it despite Maurelle's attempts at destruction. She'd never been the type of little girl to pore over wedding magazines or imagine the details of her reception, but if she had, it wouldn't have been this—a royal wedding. Claire didn't care about the flowers, the decorations, or even her gown. . But the most important part—her Ethan—well, she couldn't have dreamed of a better man. Ethan was loving, strong, faithful, and handsome. And today, he would become hers forever. She might have to pinch herself to believe it.

A guard opened the carriage door for her and waited as she exited. Once she stepped out, Claire straightened her shoulders and turned, waiting for her granny to join her.

"These crazy clothes are going to do me in." Her granny huffed and puffed as she struggled to scoot across the carriage seat.

Claire smirked. "You can't wear a tracksuit to a royal wedding."

"Who says I can't? I have that sequined one. I don't care if you're the queen of England, Amorley, or anywhere else. You're still my granddaughter, and I raised you, so I don't understand why I can't wear what I like."

Claire tilted her head. "Granny, please."

Granny waved off her granddaughter's admonishment. "Oh, I'm kidding—sort of. We need to do something to lighten the mood. All this hoopla with your stepmother has shot my nerves."

"That's over with now, so let's put it behind us and have a good day." Claire smoothed out her skirt and then offered a hand to her granny.

Granny accepted it and exited the carriage, slightly hunched over from the years of arthritis that had caused her neck and back to curve. The years were wearing on her granny. This thought brought tears to Claire's eyes.

"Why are you starting with the waterworks already? You need to save those until the music starts and you walk down the aisle."

"I was thinking about how much I love you," Claire whispered.

"I love you too, and I'm so proud of you. Now come on, let's get you hitched." Granny hooked her arm in Claire's. The pair walked to the stairs of the building where she'd had her coronation.

Claire lifted the bottom of her gown, careful not to

hook her heel inside it. There could be no mishaps today. At least with Maurelle in custody, that eliminated one potential source of problems, right?

Granny kissed her cheek before releasing her. "Well, I guess that's my cue to find my seat. It looks like they've sent a handsome fellow to escort me down the aisle." Claire turned and glimpsed the twenty-something gentleman in a suit who wore a nervous expression on his face. He hooked his finger around the collar of his neck and tugged at it.

Granny sent him a wink.

Stifling a giggle, Claire nodded. "Yeah, I guess you'd better go. Try to behave. I'll see you up there." She watched as her granny latched onto the young man's arm tighter than necessary. Shaking her head, Claire chuckled.

The doors to the abbey remained closed as she waited for her cue to enter. Claire heard the booming, majestic chords of an organ welcoming her down the aisle from within the building.

The wooden doors swung open, and Claire straightened her posture and lifted her head high. She pulled in a deep breath and released it slowly, tightening the grip on her bouquet. Then, she took the first step toward the rest of her life.

As she marched carefully but surely, her eyes settled on Ethan's.

Ethan had never looked so handsome. He wore a black suit with tails and a bowtie. Claire had seen him in dress attire for several royal dinners, but somehow, he appeared different today. He looked like the future king of Amorley. His kind eyes danced, and his smile warmed her heart. She couldn't wait to become his wife and spend the rest of her life with him. After what seemed like an eternity, she joined him at the front of the abbey near the altar.

The minister stood next to them and raised his arms in the air. The wide sleeves of his robe flapped as he gestured. "I would like to ask everyone to please take a seat. Welcome to this blessed event where we will join Queen Claire Thomson, daughter of the late king Alexander Evercliff and the late Mona Thomson of Boston, with Lord Ethan Kane, son of The Kanes of Abbingdon."

The minister fell silent as everyone took their seats, and a rustling filled the void from people adjusting dresses and setting purses on the ground. He then continued, "Marriage is a covenant created by God to join this man and this woman in a holy union for the rest of their lives. It is not something that one should enter into without sincere consideration. As such, if anyone has a reason for why these two people should not be united here today, speak now or forever hold your peace."

The rear church doors flung open at that moment, and a commotion of voices filled the air.

Claire squinted, trying to make out the figure at the rear of the church creating the ruckus.

"I object," called the voice from the back of the church.

Ethan whipped around.

Claire's jaw tightened. She glanced at the minister, waiting to see his response.

The minister raised his hand, trying to quiet the room. It seemed to produce the opposite effect as the murmuring and whispering grew to a low roar among the guests. "Please, if I may have silence for a moment. You, sir—" He pointed to the gentleman in the rear of the room, "in the back, what is your name?"

"My name is Lord Edward Smythe Chicanery. I object to this marriage." He stormed down the aisle to within a few feet of Claire and Ethan.

Claire pivoted in the direction of the minister.

The clergyman's face was as pale as his robe. "On…on what grounds?" he sputtered.

Lord Chicanery straightened his bowtie and ran a hand through his disheveled hair. "On the grounds that this woman has mismanaged her position as queen, and as long as she remains on the throne, this country will suffer under poor leadership, financial woes, and general disgrace."

A collective gasp passed through the crowd.

It didn't stop the interloper. "If she is married to this man today, with her current position as queen of Amorley, then that title will be solidified, and removing her from power will become nearly impossible. Please, you must not condone this union. I demand you wait until we've sorted things out with Parliament and—"

At that moment, the abbey doors burst open once again. This time what looked like the entire police force stampeded down the aisle and into the middle of Claire's wedding.

Perfect timing. Claire had always imagined a foreign threat against her legacy and a civil protest on her wedding day. But this? *Just wait until the queen mother sees the front page of the newspaper tomorrow.*

The police chief stepped forward and grabbed one of Lord Chicanery's arms. He sent a nod to one of his men, indicating for him to take hold of the other arm.

Now restrained, Hans' father strained against his restraints, his face deepening in color. "Now, you listen to me! I won't allow you to treat me in this manner. I am Lord Chicanery of Maltenstein, and I am here pursuing the best interests of Amorley. If you don't put an immediate stop to this...civilian's...hold on the country, then—"

The police chief tightened his grip on the gentleman. "That's quite enough." He turned toward Claire and sent her an apologetic smile. "Please forgive the intrusion, Your Majesty. We had him in hand outside the abbey, but he broke free." He gave a quick, side-long glance at Lord Chicanery. "That won't happen again."

Claire opened her mouth and closed it.

Ethan spoke up for her. "We appreciate your loyalty and quick response."

After a few seconds, Claire snapped out of her stunned state. "Yes, thank you for taking care of this matter in such an expedient, albeit public, way." She should have left it at that, but Claire couldn't resist asking the question burning in her brain. Peering at Chicanery's face, she queried, "Why do you hate me so much? What did my family or I ever do to you?"

Lord Chicanery remained still and close-lipped.

Assuming he wasn't going to give her the satisfaction of an explanation, Claire turned to the minister to tell him to continue the ceremony, but before Claire could say anything further, Chicanery lurched out of the police officers' control and spat in her face.

"You don't deserve any of this. The power, the wealth, the position does not belong to someone like you—someone so…common. Maurelle and I should be leading Amorley, not you."

The police officers grabbed Chicanery and pulled him back.

Claire wiped away the spittle from her cheek. "I see. You're right about one thing."

He didn't respond but instead remained stone-faced.

"I don't deserve anything, but I don't have to be perfect or live up to your or anyone else's expectations. I am only responsible for God's opinion of me, and he has already redeemed me, even with my flaws. Because of His love for me, I can lead Amorley well. I don't have to be afraid of you or anyone else. I feel sorry for you."

Lord Chicanery didn't respond, but his glare spoke volumes.

The police chief cleared his throat. "On that note, I'll remove this gentleman from the proceedings and ensure he undergoes extradition to Maltenstein."

Claire gave a slight nod. There was nothing left to say.

Ethan reached forward and took her hand, squeezing it. He looked toward the minister. "If you don't mind, could we continue the wedding?"

The minister opened his Bible again and found his place in the ceremony before the interruption had occurred.

The police officers dragged Lord Chicanery out of the abbey, and the door shut behind them with a thud.

Ethan stared at Claire, and his eyes widened. "Now I know why I recognized Hans when I first met him."

Claire glanced at the minister and then at Ethan. "What do you mean?"

Ethan stepped closer to Claire and lowered his voice so the entire congregation didn't hear, "I remember seeing him at the ball where they announced that you would become the heir to the Crown. Also, he attended the coronation. He stood in the back of the room. I bet Maurelle, Hans, and his father had been planning this for a long time since you arrived at the castle."

Claire's stomach dropped at this thought. She'd lived alongside a constant threat for months.

Ethan gave her hand another squeeze. "It's over. Don't let them steal another moment of your joy."

Claire nodded. "Agreed." She turned to the minister. "We're ready to proceed."

A wave of murmurs carried through the crowd until the minister raised his arms again. "Please, if we could all gather ourselves, let us continue with the marriage ceremony."

Everyone settled down, and the room fell quiet once more.

Twenty minutes later, Claire and Ethan had exchanged vows, rings, and promises for the future.

The minister closed his Bible, and a wide grin spread across his face. "I am pleased to present to you Her Majesty Queen Claire Thomson and His Royal Highness Ethan Kane as husband and wife for the first time. What God brings together may we honor and not separate." He glanced at Ethan. "You may now kiss the bride."

Ethan's lips swept into a warm smile, and he turned his gaze to Claire.

Butterflies swirled around her stomach just as they had the first day they'd met.

His bright blue eyes searched her face as if he was taking in every detail of her countenance. Ethan leaned closer and whispered, "Have I told you lately how beautiful you are? I am the most blessed man to be your husband." He placed a hand on her cheek and stroked it with his thumb.

She closed her eyes and leaned into his touch, begging her senses to capture a snapshot of this perfect moment. His cologne smelled sweet yet masculine, and her pulse quickened. He loved her. He was hers—forever. Husband and wife. She opened her eyes and looked at him. "I love you, Ethan. So much. Thank you for reminding me not to be afraid."

He traced her lips with his thumb, and his touch sent a tingle down her spine. Leaning close, Ethan pressed his mouth against hers and pulled her into a deep kiss.

Just as Claire wondered if this kiss was appropriate for a royal wedding, someone in the crowd gave a loud, encouraging whistle. Her eyes flew open, and she reluctantly pulled away from her and Ethan's first married kiss. She scanned the room to find the source of the whistle, and her eyes settled on a guilty face—Granny's. Claire shook her head but could not stop smiling.

Granny shrugged and sent Claire a quick wink.

The minister gave a nod to the organist, and the slightly uncomfortable moment was interrupted by the jovial chords of the wedding recessional song.

Claire hooked her arm in Ethan's, and instead of following royal tradition and walking out ahead of him, the pair strolled down the aisle together and exited the abbey.

The horse-drawn carriage awaited them outside. Ethan entered the carriage first and then extended his hand toward Claire.

She lifted the skirt of her dress, ducked her head, and slipped into the carriage. Settling on the seat, she turned to face Ethan. "I was nervous this morning about riding in the carriage."

He raised a brow. "Oh, really? Why? Of all the things that could have gone wrong today, I wouldn't have thought the carriage ride was a top concern."

Claire ticked off on her fingers all the times that a horse had failed her. "There was the time I found you on the side of the road after you fell off your horse, the time my horse made an inappropriate...um...deposit, at the polo match, the ill-fated ride in the Dark Forest with Maurelle, oh, and let's not forget the recent thumbtack-induced race. I don't think horses and I go well together."

As if to prove her point, one of the two horses leading the carriage stomped his hoof. The other horse whinnied and snorted. *Uh-oh.* That did not sound good.

A car passed by the carriage on the other side of the street. Where had the roadblock gone that security had promised to put in place? As it whizzed by, the driver honked. The sudden blast of his horn sent Claire's horses into a tizzy. The horse that had stomped decided to take his impatience to the next level. He shot off at a canter. And they were off!

Claire could not tell if his buddy joined in of his

own volition or if the first perpetrator had dragged his partner along.

The driver must have dropped the reins because the carriage raced ahead like an out-of-control cartoon. Claire dug her fingers into Ethan's bicep as the carriage careened down the road.

Ethan grabbed her around the waist, trying to steady her in the seat while simultaneously shouting at the driver, "Do something. Stop them. Get ahold of the reins."

The driver lunged for the dangling leather pieces without much success. "I'm trying. It's not as easy as it looks. They've never done this before."

An opening in the street that led to the main intersection lay ahead. If the driver didn't stop the carriage soon, this would not end well.

Claire decided to stop being afraid and do something. "I'm going up there."

Ethan reached for her arm and tried to stop her. "You can't. You'll get hurt. I'll go."

Before he could object further, Claire crawled to the front of the carriage and through the small opening connected to the driver's bench. She righted herself, still lolling side to side, and then eyed the free reins. Counting to three, she lunged for the leather strap closest to her. Once that was in hand, she grabbed the other strap and yanked backward, and the carriage slowed, albeit a bit crooked.

This action gave the driver a chance to take the

reins from her.

He eased the reins back again, and both horses came to a complete stop this time.

Shaking, Claire pulled in a deep breath.

Ethan called from the back, "Are you all right?"

Claire didn't budge. "Ye…yes. I think." She took a quick inventory of her limbs and ensured the driver wasn't harmed. Once she confirmed that no permanent damage had occurred, she pushed through the opening once more to the back of the carriage to join Ethan. "I believe I can say with confidence this will be my last trip in or on anything horse-related."

Ethan gave a nervous chuckle. "I wholeheartedly agree."

"I'll stick with dogs. Wilson has done many things, but nearly killing me isn't one of them. I'll take muddy pawprints any day."

Ethan laughed. "Albert took more issue with the pawprints than you did."

Good ole Albie. Claire wished he could have been part of this day. Somehow, sitting in the stalled, runaway carriage seemed so ridiculous and Claire-like that she could envision the stern speech from the queen mother. Then would quickly follow the quiet reassurance from Albert that she hadn't handled the situation too badly. "Yes, he did, but deep down, I think he liked them."

Ethan took one of her hands in his and brought it to his lips. He kissed it and whispered, "I believe you're right."

Claire smiled and lifted her face upward toward his. Closing her eyes, she pressed her lips against his, melting into him completely. He wrapped his strong arms around her. She didn't want him ever to let go. At this moment, despite the danger and fear that had threatened Claire's bliss, she found herself overjoyed by God's love for her. God had sent her great love, fought her battles, and helped her conquer all her dragons. Claire couldn't imagine feeling happier than she did at this moment, married to Ethan—royally or not.

Ethan pulled his lips away from hers and gazed into her eyes. "I love you, my sweet Claire."

She grinned. "I love you, too, my brave knight."

Chapter 23

A wave of nausea swept over Claire. The back of her neck dampened, and her hands became clammy. She clasped the edge of the bathroom countertop and stared at her reflection in the mirror.

All the blood had drained from her complexion. She turned the cold water on and splashed her face with it several times. Peeking at her image once more, she focused on the water droplets making a trail down her cheeks and concentrated on taking deep breaths.

It would be okay. *Right*? Hundreds—no, thousands of women—managed this every day.

Her eyes darted to the blue and white plastic stick on the counter next to her. Maybe she hadn't read it correctly. Picking it up, she stared at the little grey window that bore a smiley face.

Claire grabbed the box from the other side of the countertop and read the directions for interpreting the results once more. Yep—frowny face, negative result; smiley face, positive test.

Dr. Claire Thomson, Queen of Amorley, wife of

Ethan Kane for a mere two months, was pregnant.

"Darling, are you all right in there? Do you think it was something you ate?" Ethan's voice called from the other side of the door that connected their master suite to the bathroom.

"N-no. It wasn't the food." Claire's hand shook as she set the box down.

Ethan's footsteps paced on the other side of the door. "Can I come in? I'm worried about you."

No time like the present to tell him. She pulled the hand towel off the rack and dabbed her face. "Uh, sure. Okay, you can come in."

He opened the door and stepped inside the bathroom. When his eyes fell upon Claire's face, he froze. "You don't look well at all. Should I take you to the hospital?"

Claire inhaled and exhaled slowly before taking a step closer to her husband. She took one of his hands in hers and met his gaze. "No, that won't be necessary. I have something to tell you."

His brow furrowed, and concern clouded his eyes. "What's wrong?"

Tears stung Claire's eyes. "Nothing's wrong. At least, I don't think so. Quite the opposite."

He squeezed her hand. "Tell me."

Claire lifted the plastic stick in the air. "I'm pregnant. We're going to have a baby."

Ethan's face broke into a wide grin, and he scooped her into his arms. He spun her around.

Claire's hand covered her mouth. "Stop, stop." She patted his shoulder, willing the spinning to cease.

He set her on her feet with care. Leaning away from her, Ethan searched her eyes for confirmation. "We're having a baby?" He raised a brow.

She put her hand to her mouth once more and nodded.

"You have made me the happiest man in the world." Ethan wrapped his arms around Claire in a protective circle. When he lifted his head, he grinned again. "I love you, Claire. We are so blessed, aren't we?"

Claire smiled up at him. "Yes, my love, we are blessed."

~

Staring at the sea of Parliament members' faces waiting for her first words as a married monarch, Claire drew in a deep breath. Patting her cheek to compose herself before opening her mouth, she exhaled. "Thank you for coming today in support of a new era in Amorley history. We will face the future with hope, integrity, and–" Gripping the edges of the podium before her, Claire choked back bile. *Nope. Don't do it. Not in front of all of these people.*

Claire glanced down at the outfit she'd selected with the utmost of care that morning. She wore a sapphire skirt and blazer and had pulled her hair up in a tidy chignon. Just hours prior she'd gazed at her reflection in the mirror and thought she looked the perfect part of the queen of Amorley for once.

"Forgive me...where was I?" Her eyes scanned the crowd for Ethan's face. Catching his gaze, he smiled at her. The encouragement from her husband spurred her onward. "As I was saying, I am confident that I'm..." *Going to be sick.* A fresh wave of nausea surged, and Claire's body rebelled. Her hand flew to her mouth urging the vile liquid to settle down. *No. Please no.* It was useless. The entire contents of her breakfast came up and landed on the stage floor in front of the head of Parliament.

His face twisted in horror and he jumped back.

A staffer crossed the stage and stopped next to the podium. She handed Claire a handkerchief and gave her an empathetic smile. "Are you all right?"

Mortified but grateful, Claire took the piece of cloth from the staffer. "Ye...yes." She wiped her mouth clean before turning to face the crowd again. "I apologize. As I was saying–"

Granny shot out of her seat in the front row. "You're pregnant, aren't you?"

A hush fell across the room.

All of the blood left Claire's face, and the room spun for a second. She grabbed the podium to steady herself. "Well, uh, I had planned to share this news in a more appropriate manner, but..." Peering at the Parliament member's shocked expressions, she swallowed hard. *Oh, who cares?* "Yes, I'm pregnant."

Granny did a little jig before rushing to the stage

and gathering Claire in a big hug.

An eruption of camera flashes filled the space. Claire released her granny and sucked in a sharp breath.

Leaning closer, her granny whispered, "Are you worried about what tomorrow's newspapers will say?"

Claire considered the question for a moment, the issue she'd dealt with ever since she'd assumed the role of queen, then shrugged. "Nah. Nobody's perfect."

The End.

Newsletter signup:
https://www.jillboyceauthor.com/contact-1

Hook for the next book:

How will Queen Claire handle the biggest surprise of her life? Can she face the pressure of new challenges to the throne while ensuring that the Evercliff lineage survives? Find out what's next for Claire in the Royal Medicine Series by staying in touch here: www.jillboyceauthor.com

Also by Jill Boyce:

Harte Broken

About the Book:

Time doesn't heal all wounds. Love does.

Amy Harte, an Emergency Medicine physician, lost her mother to cancer suddenly on the day of her residency graduation one year ago. As a doctor, she struggles with not being able to save her mother and experiencing her best day on her worst. Since then, she has turned from her relationship with God in her guilt and grief. Near the fateful day's anniversary, her father calls to tell Amy the bank may take her childhood home. Amy knows she must save the house that holds the last precious memories of her mother.

Meanwhile, Amy meets a gorgeous Christian man, Seth, who slowly restores her belief in love and God's goodness. Their happily ever after may have to wait because Dr. Mark Blakely, Amy's dashing hospital colleague, has never met a woman he couldn't woo. Still, Amy suspects Mark values the chase more than her heart. Time is running out for Amy to save her family home and release her anger and guilt. Will she discover that love, especially God's love, heals all wounds?

Buy here:

https://www.amazon.com/Harte-Broken-Dose-Love-Book-ebook/dp/B08L9MXZV5

Sneak Peek the First Chapter:

Psalm 147:3 He heals the brokenhearted and binds up their wounds.

Chapter 1
July 2, 2017, Sunday

Amy Harte stared at the brass nameplate in front of her as she knelt on the cool green lawn. She ran her fingers over the letters, tracing the precious name. Her gaze shifted to the tilted vase attached to her mother's headstone, and she reached out to straighten it. A light breeze blew past, carrying the sharp scent of freshly cut grass.

"I'm sorry, Mom. I'm so sorry." Only silence answered. She drew in a shuddering breath. Today marked an anniversary she never wanted to celebrate. One year ago, Amy had graduated from residency and fulfilled a lifelong dream to become a physician—but on that same day, she lost her mother. How does one celebrate when the best day of life is also the worst?

Guilt washed over Amy as she reflected on how she'd let her mother down. She'd missed being with her when she passed and still carried the burden of failure to save her mom despite being a physician tasked with healing others.

The phone call Amy had received earlier that morning from her father rose in her thoughts. "Hello," she'd mumbled.

"Amy? Did I wake you?" Her father's low-timbered voice bellowed.

"Dad, are you okay?" Amy rubbed the sleep out of her eyes and tried to gain her bearings.

"Yes," her dad's voice trailed off.

"What's going on?" The last year's events flashed through her mind, and she felt a rock developing in the pit of her stomach.

"It's about the house. I got a call Friday morning from the bank and met with the manager."

Amy ran a hand through her hair, relaxing a bit. "Dad, you haven't had a mortgage in years."

"Well, that's true. We did pay it off a few years ago."

"Okay, so then what's the problem?"

"The problem is that because of the cost of your mom's treatments and then the funeral, I had to take out a second mortgage on the house. I didn't know what else to do…"

She frowned. "So, what does this mean? Can't we ask the bank for an extension? I'm sure they'll understand."

"They understand, but that doesn't change the fact that the bill is due. The bank manager said that I have sixty days to come up with the rest of the loan, $50,232, or the house will go to foreclosure," his voice cracked.

She could tell he was close to tears. "Oh, Dad. Don't cry. We'll figure something out." Amy wracked her brain, calculating her student loan balance, which teetered over the six-figure mark, and considered her rent and car payment.

She just started working at Metropolitan
Hospital, so her savings account was anemic.

"They can't take your home." She'd had tea parties
there with her mother. It was where she had learned to ride a
bike and gotten ready for prom. "Where would you live?"
Amy tried to conceal the rising panic in her voice.

"Don't worry about me. The money from my pension
more than covers my monthly living expenses, and I'm sure I
could find something reasonable to rent."

"No. Absolutely not. We lost mom. We can't
lose the family home."

"Well, if you come up with a way to make fifty-grand
in the next sixty days, let me know. Otherwise, I think it
would be a good idea if you came over in the next few weeks
to go through things."

"Don't start packing up yet, Dad. I love you." Amy
hung up and made a silent vow to save her childhood home.

A butterfly landed on her hand, snapping Amy out of
the memory. Hot tears stung her eyes, and a single droplet
rolled down her cheek. She wiped it away and shook her
head. No time for tears today. She stood and brushed tiny
blades of grass off her faded mint-green scrub pants.

A grey-haired older gentleman dressed in overalls
stood a few feet away, raking mulch into a flowerbed.
"You've got to receive God's forgiveness sometime, young
lady." He continued his work as he spoke, not lifting his
head.

Amy stood straighter and pressed her lips into a firm
line. "Excuse me, what did you say?"

The stranger halted his task and rested his arm on the
rake. His eyes found Amy's. "I said, you're going to have to
accept God's forgiveness…only way to move forward. Guilt

will eat you up inside and make it hard to love and live." The man shrugged and resumed his work as if never a word was spoken.

Her mouth fell open. *What does he know about God's forgiveness? He's probably crazy.* She started to refute his intrusion, but her pager beeped, reminding her to get moving. She walked to her car and hopped inside.

The muggy summer air, combined with choking grief, made breathing difficult. She cranked up the air conditioning and drove across town, arriving at the parking lot of Scottsburg, Virginia's community hospital. She stopped the car, stamped down the emergency brake, and paused. "Come on, Amy. Get it together. You're a professional." She slid out of the car and walked toward the hospital with hurried steps.

Straightening her shoulders, Amy stepped past the main glass doors of Metropolitan Hospital and entered the five-star, luxury-hotel-like foyer. Despite the crystal chandelier hanging overhead and a white marble floor below, the classic scent of bleach revealed it to be a well-endowed medical facility with an expansive, wealthy board of directors and donors.

Amy strode into the Emergency Department and sent a nod to her best friend and lead respiratory therapist. "Hey Beth, how's it looking today? Swamped already?"

Beth, petite with shoulder-length blond hair, leaned against the central nursing station, the main activity hub. She flicked her hand with a quick wave and grinned. "Hey, Amy!" Glancing at the large whiteboard filled with patients' names and room assignments confirmed her assessment.

Blowing her bangs out of her eyes, Beth nodded her head. "Yeah, it's been a madhouse. I thought people slept in on Sundays."

"I suppose some people use Sundays to get things done. You know... laundry, dishes, late brunches, grocery store runs... or go to church, I guess."

Some people, but not Amy. Tears threatened to spill over again, but she turned her head away and forced them back down. She held her breath. A gentle hand settled on her arm, and

Amy met Beth's sympathetic eyes.

"Hey, do you need to go home? I know this must be a hard day for you. If you want, I can tell them you didn't feel well."

She gulped in a fresh breath of air and exhaled. Amy shook her head. "No, I'm fine." As she reached for a chart, the overhead paging system announced an incoming emergency.

An ambulance siren blared, and two EMTs burst through the ED's double doors.

Amy rushed toward them.

The first medic rattled off statistics. "Victim is Brian Broadstone, driver in a two-car motor vehicle accident. He suffered a head trauma and suspected concussion, with a laceration to the right scalp. Vitals are stable."

She shifted her eyes from the patient to the medic. "Thanks, I'll take it from here." She grabbed her stethoscope from her neck and began her exam. After finding the patient in stable condition, she sent him to get a head CT.

The emergency department double doors parted again, and a tall, handsome man with dark brown hair burst through them. His eyes widened as he saw Brian's stretcher roll away.

"Hey, where's my brother going?"

He wore a black short sleeve t-shirt stretched snugly across his broad chest and thick shoulders and flattered his fit physique. His chiseled jaw clenched, and concern clouded his chestnut eyes.

Amy's cheeks warmed, and she blinked hard. *Pay attention.* She shook her head, gathering her thoughts. "Hi, I'm Dr. Amy Harte. Your brother's stable, but I sent him off for imaging. A head injury warrants a thorough workup. Were you in the car with him?" She smiled, hoping to ease his worry.

"Yeah, sorry I'm late. I rode over in the ambulance but stepped outside for a minute to call my dad. I didn't want my parents to hear about the accident from someone else."

Nodding her head, Amy understood. She knew how Scottsburg's rumor mill operated.

The handsome man met Amy's gaze, and his serious expression relaxed as he took a few steps closer. "Is he going to be okay?"

"I think he'll be fine, but I don't want to miss anything. Are you okay? We can evaluate you, too."

"I'm fine. Not a scratch on me." He stretched his hand toward Amy. "I should introduce myself. My name is Seth."

She shook his hand, and a shiver traveled down her spine at his touch. Releasing his grip, she cleared her throat. "Nice to meet you. If your brother's tests are normal, then he may be able to go home tonight as long as someone stays with him." Amy attempted to keep her tone even and professional. "Where were you guys headed so early this morning?"

The good-looking stranger grinned and shifted his weight. "Well, this week is our mother's birthday, so we were headed to grab breakfast, then take in the early church service so we'd have time to get things together afterward for her big day."

She raised her brow. "Did you make it to breakfast?"

Seth shook his head. "No, we didn't. Come to think of it, I'm starving. Do you think I have time to run to the cafeteria and grab something before Brian gets back?"

Amy smiled and nodded. "Sure. That's fine. I'll let him know where you went. If you're like me, it's hard to function before coffee."

Seth nodded. "Same." Seth searched her face, his eyes warm with interest. "Would you like a cup? I'll bring you one back."

Amy's cheeks burned, and her palms grew damp. Her fingertips tingled. She longed to say yes, but she feared that the names on the whiteboard were multiplying by the minute.

Someone tapped her on the shoulder. She turned, and Dr. Mark Blakely stood with two foam cups in hand.

Mark wore a confident grin as he eyed Seth. "No worries. I've got it covered." He passed one of the cups to Amy.

She hesitated, then accepted it. "Thanks, Mark."

Disappointment flashed across Seth's face for a moment. "Okay. Thanks again for taking great care of my brother." He smiled and reached out to shake Amy's hand again. "I'll be right back." Seth turned and walked away.

Mark left Amy's side to attend to another incoming patient.

Amy wished she could have talked to Seth longer, but Mark had impeccable timing.

Mark asked her out on a date weekly, despite her lack of encouragement. She suspected Dr.

Blakely's dating record included most of the female population of Scottsburg.

Amy approached Beth standing at the nursing station and noticed an unmistakable smirk on her best friend's face. "So, I see you've met the new Chief Financial Officer."

Exhaling for the first time in a minute, Amy asked, "What do you mean?"

Beth's grin widened, and she crossed her arms in front of her chest. "Seth Broadstone. The charge nurse told me your patient's brother is the new CFO of the hospital. Apparently, he started a few weeks ago. So, this should be interesting. I saw the look between the two of you."

She winked.

Amy rolled her eyes. "I don't know what you're talking about...there was no look. Besides, right now, I don't have time to date anybody. I have a lot on my mind." Her thoughts drifted to the conversation she'd had with her dad about her parent's house. "I'm channeling all my energy into work." She owed it to her mom.

Beth's face fell, and she grew serious. "Hey, I get it. Your work is your life...but don't forget to make time for some fun, too. I guess we hadn't met Seth yet because he's stationed on the floor with the administrators."

Shrugging in nonchalance, Amy agreed, "You're probably right." She secretly hoped this wouldn't be the last time their paths crossed.

Author Biography:

Jill writes inspirational romantic fiction with a medical theme. She is an Amazon best-selling author and the first two novels in her Royal Medicine Series, Royally Confused and Royally Engaged are 2022 Selah Award Finalists. She has also won Firebird Book Awards for Harte Broken, Perfectly Imperfect, A Prescription for Beauty, and Royally Confused.

Her debut novels are part of the *A Dose of Love* series. Each story can stand alone, but all feature strong female leads facing challenging life circumstances while finding love along the way. Jill's love of romance and her experience of losing her mother on the same day of her daughter's birth inspired the first novel, *Harte Broken*. It raises the question, "What happens when the best day is also the worst one?"

Royally Confused, Book One in the *Royal Medicine Series* introduces Claire Thomson, the heroine physician who must discover her worth by finding out her true identity. Jill enjoys royal romances and wanted to create a contemporary world filled with classic fairy-tale characters—a knight in shining armor, an evil Queen, and yes, a princess. Of course, Claire slays her own dragons and learns she comes from the one true King, her heavenly Father, who declares her worthy and loved. This series will follow the characters forward in the fictional royal world of Amorley.

Jill is a physician and mom, who loves coffee, travel, and anything glittered. She treasures spending time with her husband and children, who are her heart and greatest joy.

Let's stay in touch! Follow me on:

Facebook to enjoy #fun, faith, hope…and a little coffee!
Jill Boyce, Author, LLC

Check out my website— www.jillboyceauthor.com to join my monthly newsletter and hear about my puppy's latest hijinks, new releases, discounts, giveaways, and other great deals!

Connect with me on Twitter or Instagram as well!

Join me on Goodreads and BookBub to find out what I'm reading!

Books by Jill Boyce

A DOSE OF LOVE SERIES

Harte Broken (Book One)
Perfectly Imperfect (Book Two
A Prescription for Beauty (Book Three)

ROYAL MEDICINE SERIES

Royally Confused (Book One)
Royally Engaged (Book Two)

Royally Engaged
By
Jill Boyce

"I am the vine; you are the branches. If you
remain in me and I in you, you will bear much fruit;
apart from me you can do nothing." John 15:5 (NIV)

Prologue

Claire Thomson stared at the engagement ring on
her left hand. She twisted it between her thumb and first
finger of her right hand, sliding the ring up and down.
Pulling it off, she glanced at her naked finger where the
ring had resided. Shifting her eyes, she looked over the
lake next to Evercliff Castle.

Claire let her gaze settle on the crystal blue water
spotted with green lily pads topped with white flowers.
Would the wedding happen?

Storm clouds gathered overhead, and the wind
kicked up, carrying the scent of impending rain with it.
The sky darkened, and the weight of the cumulus
clouds mirrored the heaviness Claire carried on her
shoulders. A loud crack of lightning reverberated
through the air, interrupting her thoughts. Claire rose
and dusted bits of grass off her linen skirt.

"Come on, Wilson," she called to her golden retriever puppy, "let's go."

He stood and grabbed a stick he'd found. The piece of wood twice his size hung out both sides of his mouth, but it couldn't hide his grin.

Planting her hands on her hips, Claire tilted her head. "You look pretty pleased with yourself. I don't know how you're going to carry that back to the castle—not to mention that there's no way Albert's going to let you through the door with it."

The puppy's jaw tightened around the stick.

She shook her head. "Okay, you can bring it with you, but don't blame me if Albert takes it away from you." She headed toward the castle as tiny raindrops fell from the sky. She had so much to do and not enough time to accomplish everything—the wedding, the coronation, and her medical responsibilities.

Reviewing her to-do list made Claire's head spin. She drew in a deep breath. Could she handle it? She'd have to—she had no choice. Besides, Mona Thomson had drilled one thing into her daughter's mind, "Nothing ever gets done if you don't do it yourself." That, and, "You can rest when you're dead." Claire had one option—to pull herself together and make it happen. She couldn't consider the alternative. Especially not with Maurelle lurking in the wings.

A small sob escaped Claire's lips, but she tamped it down. The rain intensified, pelting Claire's face with sharp, cold droplets. Clenching her eyes, Claire wiped away the wetness. She couldn't tell where the storm's precipitation ended, and her tears began.

"Hurry, Wilson." She waved to the puppy and pried the stick from his mouth. Then, she scooped him into her arms and ran the rest of the way to the castle. Her legs burned, screaming in protest at the spontaneous activity. Claire tightened her jaw. She couldn't quit, couldn't rest, couldn't fail. No—she'd somehow find a way to handle it all. Somehow.

Chapter 1
May

Claire spun around, her eyes searching desperately for the book that ran her life—her planner. She didn't maintain organization in many arenas—cooking, housekeeping, or just about any other domestic duty. However, when it came to her schedule and professional obligations, Claire prided herself on keeping a detailed schedule. She'd never missed a dental appointment, work deadline, or a mail hold. Never—until now.

She sighed and rubbed her hand across her forehead. Closing her eyes, she willed her memory to bring into view the last location of the beloved itinerary keeper. Nothing. Nada.

A hand settled on Claire's shoulder.

She jumped, startled by the unexpected touch. Gasping, Claire whipped around and found the culprit. "Granny, you nearly gave me a heart attack. Don't sneak up on me like that. Give a grumble or clear your throat—something."

A teasing twinkle appeared in Granny's eyes. "Where would the fun be in that? Then, you wouldn't have gasped and made that face. You looked like Old Lady Pearl after I won the final game of Bingo last summer. Boy did that surprise her—her mouth hung open like a cod." Granny smacker her hand on her knee and guffawed. "Oh, I loved it."

Claire found her breath again and chastised her granny, "That's not nice. You know Pearl is not well. You shouldn't be glad that you shocked her."

Granny scrunched her nose and crossed her arms in front of her chest. "Pshaw. She's fine. She's not that old—no older than me. You won't let me have any fun. What's gotten you worked into a tizzy?"

Scanning the room again, Claire prayed the book might appear suddenly on the desk in her bedroom—as if it'd been there all along and she'd simply overlooked it. Nope. "I'm trying to find my planner. It has everything in it—my clinic and surgical schedule, ideas I had for the hospital's charity, and a to-do list from the queen mother for Coronation Day. That's the one I'm most upset about because she already thinks I don't take this royal stuff seriously. If I tell her I've forgotten all the things she wanted me to do for the coronation, it's going to reinforce this belief." Claire paced back and forth across the room, chewing on her thumbnail, trying to think.

Granny stepped forward, blocking her path. "Listen here, Missy. You need to calm down. Rest. You know what that word means, right?"

Claire pressed her lips together. "Of course, I do. I don't have time for rest."

Granny narrowed her eyes. "Well, you'd better make time. You know what the Bible says about the importance of rest, don't you?"

Claire sighed but humored her granny. "What?"

"It says that you can't do anything on your own. If you try to handle all this stuff by yourself, then you're going to get rotten apples."

Raising a brow, Claire lifted her eyes to meet Granny's. "Rotten apples?"

Granny gave a firm nod. "Rotten apples. Bad fruit. Look it up—you'll see. I'm telling you the truth. You can't do all this on your own."

Claire didn't have time for nursery stories today. "Thanks, but right now, I can't worry about my fruit going bad. I've got to find that planner."

Granny opened her mouth, probably ready to give another cent or two about how Claire should live life. A knock on the door interrupted her monologue.

Claire's shoulders relaxed. "Come in," she called, thankful for a break in the lecture series from Granny.

Ethan Kane, Claire's dashing fiancé, former Earl of Abbingdon, and swoon-worthy Christian gentleman extraordinaire, opened the door and stuck his head through the crack.

A smile flew to her lips, and immediately her worries lightened. Ethan always had that effect on her. He made everything better. "Ethan, did we have plans? I wouldn't be surprised if I'd missed them, because I can't find my—"

"Planner," Ethan interrupted, lifting the treasured book with one hand and opening the door a bit wider.

Claire rushed over and threw her arms around his neck. Squeezing tight, before releasing him from her death hold, she shouted, "Thank you, thank you, thank you. You saved me."

He shrugged and sent her a warm smile, his blue eyes taunting her. "Let me guess. You were in here freaking out because you didn't know every minute of every day for the next week."

She pouted. "Hey, I'm not that bad. I have a tight schedule with everything happing in the next few months. I don't know how I'm going to get it all done, but having this," she snatched the book from his grip and waved it in the air, "helps a ton. Seriously, thank you."

Granny sidled up behind Claire and whispered in her ear, "You don't need that thing. It's going to make you sick. Bad fruit. Remember what I said." Then, she turned to Ethan. "Young man, it's always a pleasure to see you. I'm guessing you two will want to take a stroll, hold hands, and be romantic, so I'll skedaddle." She walked past the couple but turned in the doorway before leaving, settling her gaze on Claire. "Bad. Fruit." Then, she walked down the hallway, probably on her way to tease and torment Albert about the lunch menu.

Ethan sent Claire a quizzical look. "What's with the obsession about fruit?"

Claire shook her head. "It's nothing. Granny's in one of her moods where she feels the need to impart ancient wisdom to me. She's done it ever since I was a kid. Granny always harped on me to wear a coat when I went outside so I wouldn't catch a cold. In medical school, I found out that wasn't true. She means well, but I don't place a ton of weight on her weird advice—like avoiding bad fruit."

He shrugged and accepted her answer. "Okay." Lifting his hand, he waved her over. "Come here. I want to tell you something."

She arched a brow and took a few steps closer to the man who had captured her heart and filled it with love. "What do you want to tell me?" The corners of her lips tugged upward.

He leaned his head down next to her ear and whispered, "I love you, Dr. Claire Thomson, and I can't wait to marry you." He turned his face and pressed his lips against her cheek, letting them linger for a moment before pulling away. He sent her a smile and shoved his hands in the pockets of his pressed khaki shorts. The sapphire blue polo shirt he wore complimented his eyes.

She met his gaze, and her heart pounded harder. "I love you, too. I can't wait for the wedding either, but how do you feel about becoming a king?" Flicking her eyes down at the planner in her hands, the weight of the upcoming months weighed upon her.

Money and position didn't matter to Ethan. However, a nagging worry circled Claire's mind that he wouldn't want the royal life and all the expectations involved with it. She frowned.

Ethan stepped forward and placed a gentle hand under her chin. "I want you. I'm ready to do whatever it takes to be with you, even if it means wearing a crown. Besides, it will drive Richard crazy, so that's a perk." He chuckled and gave her a quick peck on the lips.

Claire shook her head. "You're terrible. You can't lord your title over your brother." She paused, considering all the manipulative and vengeful things Richard had done or said. "Well, maybe a little lording…but only a little." She laughed and opened her planner. "Okay, now that you've found my life again, I've got to figure out how I'm going to accomplish everything in the next few months."

Claire flipped the pages forward and stopped on today's date. **"There's** not much time—not much time at all." She tapped her foot, running through all the things to do and the calls to make. "Oh, and don't forget, somewhere wedged in the middle of the next few weeks will be Oxmund Hospital's charity luncheon. I promised them I'd help plan it and give a speech—you know how I feel about public speaking."

Ethan's lips curved upward, and he stifled a laugh. "Oh, I know. Don't think I've forgotten the polo match."

She gave him a playful shove on the arm. "Hey, don't tease me. I couldn't help it that I dropped the microphone in a horse's, well, you know. I was nervous. Super nervous. I'm not sure any amount of royal lessons from the queen mother can fix that problem."

He rubbed her arms with his hands and squeezed her. "You'll do great."

She sent him a half-grin. "I don't have as much faith as you do, but I'll do my best." She peered at her planner and flipped back to today's date. Tapping the page riddled with pen marks and words circled in highlighter, she reminded him, "See. Today—lunch with the queen mother. I knew there was something important I had to do today. She wants to review the next week's activities and preparations for the coronation. You should join us." She closed the book and clutched it to her chest like a child's favorite toy.

He raised his brow and rubbed his chin, which had a day's worth of stubble. "I don't know... I'm not dressed for lunch with your grandmother, and I didn't even shave today. Are you sure she won't mind?"

"I'm sure. Please. Feeding you lunch is the least I can do for my valiant knight who rescued my planner from the dungeon of lost items." She placed the back of her hand to her forehead and feigned a damsel in distress pose.

He laughed and shook her head. "You're more like Granny than you know. Okay, you've got yourself a date. Let's have lunch with the queen mother and talk about all things coronation."

She hooked her arm in his and followed him out of the bedroom. "Can you think of any better way to spend your day?"

He glanced down at her as they walked and grinned. "I cannot."

Neither could Claire.

He kissed the top of her head and led her down the stairs and toward the grand banquet room to plan their future.

For the first time today, hope filled Claire's chest. She could do it all. In a few months, she'd become queen of Amorley, Mrs. Ethan Kane, and the proud owner of her own happily ever after.

Made in the USA
Middletown, DE
04 May 2022